VICTOR

MORDICAI GERSTEIN

Victor

A novel
based on the life of
the Savage of Aveyron

Frances Foster Books · *Farrar, Straus and Giroux* · *New York*

Library of Congress Cataloging-in-Publication Data

Gerstein, Mordicai.

    Victor : a novel based on the life of Victor, the Savage of Aveyron / Mordicai
Gerstein.— 1st ed.

        p.   cm.

    "Frances Foster books."

    Summary: A novel based on the work of Dr. Jean Marc Itard who spent the years
shortly after the French Revolution working with a "savage" boy whom he called Victor,
trying to prove he was not an idiot and to teach him how to live in human society.

    ISBN 0-374-38142-9

    1. Itard, Jean Marc Gaspard, 1775–1838—Juvenile fiction. 2. Wild Boy of
Aveyron—Juvenile fiction. [1. Itard, Jean Marc Gaspard, 1775–1838—Fiction. 2. Wild
Boy of Aveyron—Fiction. 3. Feral children—Fiction. 4. France—History—1789–1815—
Fiction.] I. Title.

    PZ7.G325Vi   1998

    [Fic]—dc21   97-44863

Translation of selection from Rainer Maria Rilke's *Sonnets to Orpheus* by Jan Swafford.

For my mother, Faye

ACKNOWLEDGMENTS

François Truffaut's haunting 1970 film *The Wild Child* introduced me to the story of Victor. I later read the two compelling reports by Victor's teacher, Jean-Marc-Gaspard Itard, on his work with the boy, and was inspired to retell the story, first as a picture book, and then as a novel. I found Itard's reports in Lucien Malson's book, *Wolf Children and the Problem of Human Nature*, and also in a translation by George and Muriel Humphrey entitled *The Wild Boy of Aveyron*. Harlan Lane's *The Wild Boy of Aveyron*, the most complete, perceptive, and readable account of the case, was also an essential source for *Victor*, as were parts of his *When the Mind Hears*. I am grateful to Mr. Lane, as well, for his generous help in locating additional source material. Roger Shattuck's *The Forbidden Experiment* was also useful.

Michelle Bacholle translated for me some of the material that was in French, as did Catherine Iselin, whose work gave me access to Thierry Gineste's *Victor de l'Aveyron*, another authoritative work on the subject.

Throughout the extended period of the novel's writing, I enjoyed the encouragement, astute readings, and indispensable support of my wife, Susan Yard Harris. I was also blessed with the advice of friends and fellow writers Carol Edelstein, Tony Giardina, Betsy Hartmann, Joann and Howard Kobin, Zane and Norman Kotker, Marissa Labozzetta, John Stifler, and Jan Swafford, with all of whom I shared the manuscript in progress. The unflagging support and enthusiasm of my agent, Joan Raines, helped to dispel doubts and kept me at my task. And to my editor, Frances Foster, goes my gratitude for initiating and guiding the process that made the manuscript into the book.

August 1997   M.G.

When the leaders of the French Revolution formed the First Republic, they believed it was an event that surpassed in importance the birth of Christ. Along with discarding their king and queen they tossed out the calendar used throughout the Western world and created a new *Revolutionary* calendar. September 22, 1792, the day the Republic was founded, became the first day of the year I, and in France, time began anew.

The Revolutionary calendar had twelve new months, each containing three ten-day weeks. The months were named by a poet revolutionary:

Vendémiaire (the grape harvest) · *September 22 to October 21*
Brumaire (the misty month) · *October 22 to November 20*
Frimaire (the month of frost) · *November 21 to December 20*
Nivôse (the month of snow) · *December 21 to January 19*
Pluviôse (the rainy month) · *January 20 to February 18*
Ventôse (the windy month) · *February 19 to March 20*

Germinal (when seeds sprout) · *March 21 to April 19*
Floréal (the blossoming month) · *April 20 to May 19*
Prairial (the month to mow meadows) · *May 20 to June 18*
Messidor (the month of harvest) · *June 19 to July 18*
Thermidor (the month of heat) · *July 19 to August 17*
Fructidor (the month of fruit) · *August 18 to September 16*

This left five days to be celebrated as new holidays with the names Genius, Work, Virtue, Reason, and Reward.

The story of Victor begins just a year before Napoléon Bonaparte seized power on Brumaire 18, the year VIII (November 9, 1799), and declared the Revolution over. Under his authoritarian rule the last of the Revolution's idealism, as well as its murderous fanaticism, faded away. Napoléon revoked the Revolutionary calendar, and on January 1, 1806, France rejoined the chronology of the Western world. The "rational," symmetrical Revolutionary calendar, with its poetically named months and roman-numeral years, vanished like a historical soap bubble.

The story of Victor, which is also the story of his teacher, Jean-Marc-Gaspard Itard, and his great experiment in education, takes place within that bubble.

Succulent apple, pear and banana,
gooseberry . . . All of these speak
death and life into the mouth . . . I sense . . .
read it on the face of a child,
tasting them. This comes from afar.

Rainer Maria Rilke, *Sonnets to Orpheus*

To his Excellency the Minister of the Interior

My Lord:

To tell you of the Wild Boy of Aveyron is to recall a creature forgotten by those who saw him merely as a passing novelty, and scorned by those who thought to judge him. As for me, who has watched his progress and cared for his needs, always indifferent to the forgetfulness of some and the contempt of others, five years of careful, daily observation have enabled me to present to Your Excellency the report you await . . . Please believe that if not for your formal request, I would have gladly kept silent and abandoned to oblivion a story which is less an account of a student's progress, and more the history of his teacher's failure.

Jean-Marc-Gaspard Itard,
A Report on the Progress of Victor of Aveyron, 1806

VICTOR

I

The baker and his wife saw it from their shop window.

Two woodcutters, one behind the other, bundles of sticks on their backs, marched out of the early morning mist. Between them, on their left shoulders, they carried a horizontal pole with something hanging from it. From across the little square it looked like some kind of animal tied by its four legs. A wild pig? A small, scrawny bear?

"What the hell is that?" the baker muttered. He peered through the eddying mist and squinted a moment or two before his mouth dropped open.

"My God!" said his wife. "It's a child!"

They ran out for a closer look. A dozen others from shops around the square did the same. The sun flared over the eastern ridge and burned away the mist. The cobbles shone with golden light.

Hung from the pole slid between its bound wrists and

ankles, and naked except for layer upon layer of crusted dirt and filth, the child looked like something dug out of the earth: an overgrown forked turnip or potato. A great tangle of mud-plastered hair, snarled with twigs, leaves, and other forest debris, framed a smeared, grimy face with gleaming, dark brown eyes. The people closest could see that it was a boy. Blinking, his mouth slightly open, he stared upward. His shining eyes reflected the huge white clouds that now rolled across the blue overhead.

"Where did you find him?" asked the baker.

One of the woodcutters pointed above the stone church to a mountain that looked close enough to touch. The town was surrounded by mountains and was made of stone. It looked as if it had been carved from the hills by the slow abrasions of wind, rain, snow, and the passing years, all of which now seemed to be wearing it away, erasing it.

"We were just below the ridge in the oak grove," said one woodcutter.

"Feeling our way through the fog," said the other, "—you know you can't see much past your nose these spring mornings—and *bang*! There he is. As close as you. We stare at him. He stares at us and—*poof*! There he goes like a rabbit!"

"We chase him around the trees," said the first. "He starts up one and I grab his ankle. He puts up a hell of a fight. Look here . . . and here!" He showed the still-oozing scratches and tooth-shaped gouges through tears in his bloody shirt, and enjoyed the gasps of the crowd.

"Twisting, clawing, kicking, biting. Finally, I sit on him till Raymond can get the rope around him."

"He was trembling all over!" said Raymond, fluttering his hands. "We tried to pull him after us." Raymond shrugged. "He wouldn't come."

"So we cut the pole," said the other, "and here he is."

"Who is he?" asked the butcher. "Does anybody recognize him?"

"Hah!" laughed his wife. "Under that hair and dirt he could be our Eugène! I never saw anything so filthy!"

They slid the pole from between the boy's hands and feet and put him down against the stone ledge of the ancient Roman fountain in the center of the square. Topped with its four little greenish-bronze men—the Little Romans they were called—each faced smirking in one of the four directions, each with his enormous member spouting into the stone basin below, the fountain had been here since before the land was called France and was the town's sole distinction. The boy huddled his back against it, still bound at the ankles and wrists, and hugged his legs. He began rocking, back and forth, side to side, and from his throat came a soft guttural hum—*hnn hn, hnn hn*—two notes repeated over and over. His eyes were open and shining but he seemed to look at nothing. People crowded around and stared; some spoke to him, some shouted. He seemed not to hear, as if he were listening to someone else, watching something they couldn't see.

"What's your name, boy?"

"Can you talk? Has anyone heard him say anything?"

"He must be . . . what? . . . eight? Ten at the most."

"Has he got a tongue? Open his mouth!"

"Open your mouth, boy!" The baker and butcher squeezed his mouth open. Surrounded by yellow-brown teeth, his tongue was pink and wet.

"He's blind for sure," said one of the woodcutters. "Look . . . I wave my hand . . . nothing!"

"He must be deaf, too," said a heavy man, the acting mayor and the owner of the inn. He clapped his hands near the boy's ear. The boy didn't blink or twitch, but continued his rocking, his ceaseless, monotonous humming.

"Deaf! Stone deaf!" everyone agreed. The baker and his wife squatted near the boy and offered him bread. Without looking, he sniffed at it for a moment, then ignored it.

"He doesn't like your bread," said the innkeeper.

"Or," said the baker, a sinewy man dusted with flour, "he doesn't know what it is."

"Watch out!" screamed the baker's wife. She jumped back with raised skirts as liquid spouted from between the boy's legs and splattered the cobblestones.

"A little Roman!" she laughed along with the others. "He's not housebroken, that's the one sure thing!"

"Either he's a runaway lunatic," said the innkeeper, "or someone lost him on purpose, one of the hill people's idiot bastards."

"Why the hills?" asked the baker's wife. "Why not the town?"

They all looked at each other and nodded. Why not, indeed?

"No!" grunted the baker.

"What do you mean, 'no'?"

"Look at him. He's not blind. He's a woods child. I've heard for years there's been one up there somewhere. Raised by wolves maybe."

"More likely pigs," quipped the innkeeper.

"Do you know the hermit up near Marusson?" asked the butcher's wife. "The one with the goat cheese? He told me he saw such a child just over a year ago."

"Could be," conceded the innkeeper. "It doesn't keep him from being a loony or an imbecile-bastard."

"Imbecile, *pah*!" said the butcher. "He's been in the hills for months. All that freezing weather we had. I'd like to see you last *one* night up there. Naked."

"Months, hell! He's been up there for *years*!" the baker insisted vehemently. "He doesn't even know what bread is! Remember . . . what's his name? Gabelle! His little boy disappeared during the uprising in '93. Why couldn't it be him?"

"Yes . . ." said the butcher's wife. "Or my cousin Edouard's boy that went missing in Toulon during the siege. Look at his eyes; he isn't blind. And he's no idiot."

"Here's someone who'll know for sure," said the innkeeper, pointing with his chin across the square.

"Jean!" he called. "Come here! Come here, boy!"

There were chuckles as a boy of nine or ten shuffled toward them. One of his fingers was deep in his nose and he dragged an old bone on a string. With vacant eyes and open mouth, he cautiously approached the naked child and stared.

"What do you think, Jean? Is this an idiot?" asked the barkeeper. "You're the expert." Everyone laughed. Jean leaned slowly closer, peering at the boy. The boy rocked and hummed and looked through him.

"This is a bear," said Jean, solemnly nodding his head. "This is a real bear."

"More like a skunk," said someone in the crowd. There was more laughter.

An old woman with a basket came out of the church. She saw the crowd around the fountain and shuddered.

Since the Revolution six years ago, some vile things had been done in this square. She crossed herself and started down the steps. These days, few went to church: mostly old women. Many churches had been confiscated and ransacked; this one's cross knocked down, its saints burnt on these steps. Many priests were arrested and beheaded—not to mention the king! She crossed herself again. All in the name of reason. Reason, hah! She shuffled and lowered her bunioned feet from one stone step to the next. No matter, she thought. Let others do as they like. Revolutions, republics—something for the men to shout and fight about, to kill each other over. No matter; only God is real. She shuffled over to the crowd, pushed through, and saw the boy.

She stared at him for a moment. Then she shouted something. She was hoarse and toothless.

"Again, Granny," said the innkeeper. "Slower!"

"What did he do?" she croaked. "Why is he tied up? Untie him! Look, he's starving!" She began to undo the ropes.

"Careful," warned one of the woodcutters. "He'll be halfway up the mountain before you can blink." He helped untie the boy, but left a rope around his waist knotted to the hitching ring in the fountain. The old woman fumbled in her basket and, one after another, offered the boy cheese, bread, sausage, and an onion. Without looking, always rocking to his monotonous moan, he sniffed at each thing. There was no further sign of interest.

"Well, Raymond," said the butcher, clapping the woodcutter on the shoulder, "at least he doesn't eat much. What will you do with him?"

"*Oh* no!" protested Raymond, shrugging him off. "I don't know what to do with the ones I've got! You take him!"

Everyone laughed as the butcher suggested the baker, who offered the child to the innkeeper.

As the word spread, the crowd grew larger and livelier. Theories—some whispered behind the backs of hands—abounded as to whose child this might be. Several serious arguments were under way about the boy's hearing, his intelligence, his age; work was forgotten. Anything unusual, any novelty, was always welcome, but this was a windfall, a miraculous mystery, drama to transform the everyday tedium. The air was growing festive. A warm southern breeze came up. It stirred softly through the square and the crowd was startled to silence by a sound like little bells, or glass wind-chimes. It was laughter. A spritely, delighted laughter. Everyone looked around. It was the boy. He stared at the sky with sparkling eyes and laughed like a baby in a bath.

The breeze died away and the boy went perfectly still. He blinked for a moment and then, slowly, like a released metronome, the rocking resumed and the humming began. He was as before: indifferent, oblivious. Fueled by this incident, arguments flared with fresh vigor.

The only event of the day that could compete with the strange child was the midday meal, and around noon people started drifting off. It was better to discuss things over food, and serious conversation was good for the digestion. The innkeeper and the baker stood off to one side discussing what might be done with the boy. There was an orphanage in Saint-Affrique over the mountain, but how would they get him there? And who would take him? The bell clanged twelve and the doors to the school burst open.

Boys of all ages ran shouting out across the square to see this new wonder. They swarmed around him. Because the very word "naked" was a source of amusement for them, they laughed first of all at his nakedness. They asked him where his pants were. They asked him his name. When he didn't respond, they began to shout at him. "Hey, are you deaf? Don't you understand French?" He didn't look at them. Hugging his knees, he continued to rock, back and forth, to and fro, as if they weren't there. "Look!" cried one. "He's too good for us."

"Maybe he's a duke!"

"A count!"

"A prince!" The bolder ones began to poke him, and then pinch him and pull his hair. Some of the adults chuckled; some said, "Leave him alone!"

"It's a chimpanzee!" announced one boy. "It's your twin brother!" responded another. "It's yours!" "It's your sister!" As the grown-ups drifted off, one of the boys began to throw pebbles. Another darted close and slapped the child across his face. There were whoops of laughter, though the child seemed to notice nothing.

"He needs a bath!" called another boy, and, filling his mouth from the fountain, he squirted water in the child's face. When he licked his lips, others sprayed him also. The oldest of them, first glancing up at the fountain and then over his shoulder at the preoccupied adults, said, "He needs a Roman bath!" He opened his pants and aimed at the child's face. There was a unanimous shout of approval, and everyone who could crowd close enough joined in.

It was the old woman who hobbled up squawking like an enraged crow and, with an explosion of curses and blows, sent them jeering off to their various homes for dinner. She had gone to find something the child might eat. Wheezing and mumbling softly, she wiped his face, using her apron and water from the fountain. She held an apple and then a carrot under his nose, but there was no response till she showed him a baked potato. He sniffed it avidly, took it in both hands, and devoured it. The old woman cackled and clapped her hands. She patted his head.

"That's what you want, eh? All right, my sweet, my

baby! I'll be back with more." She pinched both his cheeks and squinted into his eyes. "I'll come right back. Then I'll take you home, sweetheart. I'll take him home!" she croaked to the innkeeper and the baker, both still deep in discussion.

"You want a pet, Granny?" said the innkeeper. "Can you handle him?" But she was already hurrying off for more potatoes. The two men had decided that the authorities in Saint-Sernin, the district seat, should be notified. And the old woman would look after the boy? Good. There was no hurry. They went off to their dinners.

When the old woman returned twenty minutes later, the one-o'clock bell reverberated through the stones beneath her shuffling feet. The square was empty except for Jean, the idiot boy. He sat on the fountain's rim tying his bone to the rope that had held the strange child.

"That bear ran away," said Jean. "I can untie ropes and he ran away home. Look." He dangled his bone for the old woman to inspect. "See?" he said proudly. "I can tie ropes, too. I'm a good boy."

Above him the Little Romans smirked and spouted.

2

He can move. Now he is moving. Trees and leaves and rocks fly past and under. The world is in motion. His nose points the way.

The place where he could not move was a tangle of clamoring odors—sour, bitter, sharp, stinging, fetid. They held and smothered him. He could smell nothing. No leaves, no birds, no moss. He needed to move, but could not. There were no chestnuts, no acorns, no mushrooms. There was no world.

Now he runs and the warm soft wind carries him faster and higher and no one hears his laugh. Not even him. What he hears is water. It mimics his laughter. He hears it with his tongue and his throat. His nostrils inhale its smell in huge watery gulps. Roots and rocks and mossy stones blur underfoot. He slips and tumbles, rolling and splashing into water. Water pours over his body and down his throat; he melts into water.

• • •

Smells combine, separate, and recombine. Earth and rotting leaves, fox and mushroom. He bends forward, trotting now, fingers brushing leaves and sticks aside. Here is a mushroom. Here is another. Now hunger makes the world move. Quick, clever fingers reach under fallen trees and reappear with food: acorns, nuts, and fragrant roots. Stones flipped on their backs reveal grubs, worms, and juicy beetles. Sniff every prize. If the nose approves, the mouth takes it. Sucked, bitten, and chewed, it explodes into warmth and light. Into happiness.

The blossom stink is everywhere, drowning the smells of what he needs. Hunger impels and gnaws. Claw the sun-warmed earth. Here are bulbs, sweet to the tongue, pungent, succulent. And the crisp eggs of ants.

Now, tangled in brambles, his fingers blur, and again and again, berries burst in his mouth, and the world is nothing but berries—the juice of berries, the smell of berries, and whatever is not berries is pushed aside and disappears.

Awake.
Eyes open.
Moon fills the sky. Reach out. Touch it. There is nothing between him and it. No word to separate and protect him. His face is the moon's mirror. Slowly, lifted by his eyes, he rises, sways, and begins to spin. From his open mouth a sound rises. A long, high, thin sound. He is the moon's

puppet. Wrapped in its cold light, it dances him up out of the forest, into the blackness between the stars. He hurls himself upward, arms out, to hold and embrace it, but finds himself sprawling over moss and leaves and the smooth icy stones.

Moon fills the sky. Reach out. Touch it.

Squirrels leap and scurry through rattling leaves, chasing from nut to nut. With quick little teeth they chew and watch him from the sides of their shining eyes. He does not see them; they are not food. High in the tree his fingers pull meat from husk, over and over, and the world is nothing but chestnuts. Whatever is not chestnut is tossed aside and disappears. He swells rounder and fuller till, like a chestnut, he's part of the tree he's perched in. His eyes close.

He dreams he is in a chestnut tree eating chestnuts.

Slapped awake by stinging whips of sleet, he slips, falls, scrapes down the tree, pawing the roots for a place to be into, to be under. With fingers and toes he claws from below, gathers over, burrowing under leaves and into earth, where it is quiet, dark, and still.

Eyes open. Flecks of light flutter and fall. Some touch his knees and vanish. Some float into his open mouth. He leaps up! He hears his own laughter as the sound of snowflakes. He tumbles over and over down exploding hills of snow.

He feasts on snow. He wriggles under it, springs up out of it, and falls gladly back. He whirls, and the snow whirls.

Stop.

Tiny neck-hairs bristle and shudder. He turns his head. Hunger is behind a tree. He smells it watching him. He moves away; it moves with him. Now he is the acorn, the mushroom. He is the food, the berry full of juice. He trots and hunger trots behind. Its rank odor holds and slows him. Now there is nothing but hunger, after him and running hard.

On a cedar bough high above the snow, his ears and chest pound and pulse. He peers down. Hunger circles below. It wails and calls to him with its red throat and its teeth. It mourns and croons. In the tree he yawns and yawns again.

He is awake. His growling belly wakes him. He slips and falls through snow, into snow. His belly drives him over and under snow, running, crawling, combing the icy air for shreds of scent that take him this way, that way. Here his nails tear and peel the bark. He chews it, sucks it. He rips open and devours the entrails of a frozen bird. Deep under a drift he touches the frozen body of a doe. He burrows next to it, huddles close. It feeds him.

He is awake. A breeze touches him, soft and fat, full of earth and old leaves, swelling roots, and worms. And water. The world is dripping with water.

He jumps up! He falls into the wind and the smell of water. He rolls in melting snow and warm mud, tumbling over and over down the gurgling, streaming hill.

Stop.

There is a stain in the air. A nasty streak. Something sour. Something foul and fetid. His throat and belly clench. He's up, legs pumping. The world flies past and away.

The dogs began baying and frothing as if they'd gone mad, and the three men looked up the hill. One of them shouted, and pointed at something running on the ridge. At first they thought it was a wolf, and one of them raised his rifle. Then they saw it against the sky.

"Christ! What is it?"

"Look how it runs—hind legs, then all four."

The third man made a low whistling sound. "I bet it's that wild boy they caught last spring!"

"Last spring? How did he live through that bitch of a winter?"

"Let's ask him!"

The dogs were released. They ran their game over the ridge and then down through a gully full of boulders. Snarling and barking, they ran it up a bare oak tree and then circled, hurling themselves upward and snapping their jaws. The men came puffing up and beat them back.

It took all morning to get the boy down. He had climbed till he'd run out of tree. He perched on the topmost branch, clinging to it with all his toes and fingers. He made little squealing noises, and rocked quickly back and forth, till the whole tree trembled. He stared down at the men with teeth bared in a grimy mask that looked more grief than threat. One of them climbed as close as he could. Using a long stick, while the others shouted direction and encouragement, he poked and prodded till finally the boy was forced to let go. He shrieked as he fell and the two men on the ground caught him.

He flails and kicks. Move! Everything demands movement. He claws and bites. The stinking wool, the reeking whiskers, the stench that holds him. Urine and garlic, fermented sweat, woodsmoke, and excrement. But he can't move and something vibrates through him, rattling his bones, fiercer than the fiercest hunger.

"Hold him!" grunted one of the men. "Hold him! My God! He's pissing all over himself!"

"He's scared!"

"Shit! He'd tear your face off if he had the chance! Here's the rope!"

They lost and regained their hold several times before they got the rope around the boy's wrists and ankles and threaded a stout, cut sapling between them. Two of them shouldered the pole and, with the boy swinging from it and the dogs barking, they started down the mountain to the flat little valley, back to the village of Lacaune.

3

"The Little Roman is back! The stinking Little Roman!"

The children chanted and pranced around the old woman as she took the boy's arm and stood him up. Clutching the rope tied to his waist, she mumbled in his ear and gave him little toothless kisses. She clucked and tugged at him. Hesitantly, he came.

"I should have taken you last time! I swear to God, I haven't slept since, thinking about you up there and worrying. Come, my baby, come, my sweet . . ."

He held back but she led him slowly out of the square. Laughter burst from the crowd as he left a trail of turds.

At the edge of the square, in the narrow street that led to the old woman's house, the boy suddenly began to trot, pulling her after him. The delighted crowd cheered and followed. The boy turned his head this way and that, and kept trying to run off in various directions. There were laughing faces in all of them. By the time they reached the old woman's door, sweat ran down her face and body and the breath rattling through her toothless mouth made her lips flutter. She fumbled the latch open and pulled the boy inside. The door closed and the crowd whooped with delight as he leapt halfway back out the window before the old woman caught his rope. She hauled him back in and slammed the shutters.

His mouth fills with water. In the chaos of strange smells that are not earth, not sky, there is an odd, exciting smell. He remembers it. Something fills his hands, heavy, like a sun-warmed stone. His nostrils brush the dusty, crackling thing. He opens his mouth and bites. He has no word for potato. Nothing separates him from it. He devours it.

The old woman's name is Beatrice. She has outlived a husband and three of her sons. Fevers, wars, revolutions—maybe with daughters she'd have more left. Her one surviving child moved far to the north and he's never come back. He sent a letter once. She keeps it in a drawer and takes it out from time to time; she feels the heavy paper and studies the inky marks. Sometimes she has a neighbor read it to her, though she knows every word by heart. No matter. He'll come one day. She kneels by the hearth and feels in the ashes for another potato. She sees that she has the boy's full attention. He snatches and the second potato quickly follows the first, as does a third. He eats squatting by the fireplace, and she sits beside him, crooning and muttering, smoothing his hair. He seems to be looking into the embers, but she can't be sure. He rocks slowly as he eats, from side to side, and his soft, continuous humming blends with Beatrice's creaky croon.

The canary joins in with an occasional note or a fragment of melody. It hops from swing to perch, from perch to floor, pecking at its bars.

"What do you think, Henri?" Beatrice asks it. "Isn't this a fine boy? Oh, he's just a baby yet. Still a baby. The image of Maurice. Remember Maurice? My sweet baby, my dear baby . . ." Her hoarse, sibilant mumbling rambles on like an endless prayer. Randomly, she addresses God, or the boy, or one of her children, or the canary, who is named after her late husband.

The boy no sooner finishes the third potato than he's at the door, sniffing and feeling around its edges. Then he's on the table beneath the window, his fingers fluttering over the shutters, his face pressed to them, smelling the sunlight and trying to touch it. Then to the back door, slapping at it and making small mewing noises. He scuttles round and round the room, from window to window and door to door, looking for the outside. Beatrice shuffles and wheezes after him, and finally gets hold of his hand. He follows her reluctantly, with quick little steps, never walking but always at a kind of trot.

"This is the soup pot. This is soup. Cabbage soup. This is a chair. Henri's favorite chair, wasn't it, Henri? For sitting and smoking his pipe. Oh, that smelly pipe, Henri! This is my cup. Cup, for drinking tea . . ." She shows him cabbage, and spectacles, bowls and bacon, forks, pots, onions and ladles, spoons, knives, strainers, bread, and turnips. Shears, thread, thimble, and needles. He sniffs them all and drops them. These are not food.

The boy squats suddenly, and Beatrice quickly learns that it means he is about to urinate. Defecation is harder to catch, because he does it standing, and it takes her by surprise.

"No no no no no!" she screeches, and drags him by hand and hair into the tiny courtyard, but not so far as the privy. As his urine streams over the stones, she lectures him on the use of the privy, but realizes that just to get him out of the house is enough for now. The next problem is to get him back in the house. The courtyard has a piece of sky over it; the boy sees it and is desperate to reach it.

Inside, she stands him in a large basin and, with warmed water and yellow soap, she begins to wash him. He allows her vigorous scrubbing. One by one, layers of grime dissolve—a kind of archaeology—and the scars are revealed: hieroglyphics that tell of disasters and triumphs. Cuts, burns, gashes, tears, bites; as each is uncovered, Beatrice clucks or makes little grunts of pain. She fingers them, and some she kisses, and asks Henri or God whether they've ever seen the like. Tears stream down her face. She wipes them away with the heel of her hand, but one always remains suspended from the tip of her nose.

"Oh Henri! Henri! What did they do to him? What did they do to my baby? Oh my God, dear Jesus, my babies, my babies—what did they do?" She tilts his head back and is startled by a long lightning-like scar that arcs across his throat from ear to ear.

"My God! My Jesus!" She throws both arms around him and they rock back and forth together, humming, mumbling, and croaking. Her tears drip down his back.

The boy laughs. Beatrice thinks at first it's the canary's song. Then she sees a constellation of sunbeams dancing on the wall. The boy watches them. His scrubbed face glows softly and he laughs.

His brown eyes shine beneath long, thick lashes. His nose is fine and pointed. His small, laughing mouth shows rows of teeth, perfect as kernels of dark yellow maize. The old woman laughs with him. She kneels and scrubs his hips and thighs and whoops when his pretty little "tail" stands up and sticks straight out—just like Claude!—and she washes that too, and the little pouch below, the little walnut of flesh.

"Hah! You pretty rascal you—you puppy! Look at this puppy, Henri, just like Jean-Paul at his age." She dries his face and soft brown hair. "Remember Jean-Paul? We're going to dress you, Jean-Paul. Don't you worry. Even a baby needs clothes."

It's in front. It's behind. It surrounds him. He can't get away from it. Whichever way he turns, it's there. If he pulls the front away, it traps him from behind. He spins, trying to outflank it. He pulls it up and suddenly he's buried, smothered. Terror flutters round his belly like a trapped moth. He can't move.

. . .

"Oh Maurice, Maurice! Look what he's done, Henri! All tangled and tied . . ." She takes hold of the struggling, whimpering bundle and they tip over onto her bed, where they struggle some more. Finally, having rescued him from the nightgown, she gasps, and wheezes as she smooths his hair, and quiets his small, sharp cries with kisses and then a potato, warm, fragrant, and dusty with ashes. His eyes are windows on rapture.

"Oh, what a good boy!" she beams and grins, her eyes streaming. "Oh, what a dear, good boy!"

As soon as the light has drained from the two small rooms, he stops his prowling. He curls up on the floor in a corner with his clenched fists over his eyes and his face pressed to his knees. It hurts her to see him lying there on the bare floor. She has made him a bed with a straw mattress and clean sheets, but he ignores it. He sleeps lightly. Occasionally, like a sleeping dog's, his nose or leg twitches. She sits and watches him. She rocks and mutters.

She is wakened at dawn by a small hand pulling at hers. She opens her eyes, and the sight of him fills and warms her. He pats her shoulder and, with little tugs, he looks toward the hearth, where under the ashes potatoes have spent the night.

With a rope tied from her waist to his, a hempen umbilicus, she takes him out in his new gown. He leaps into the cobbled street and all but pulls her over.

"Hey! Hey! Stop, you bad thing! Robert! Slowly, slowly!" With a large basket on her arm, she scolds and uses all her strength to hold him as he trots all the way down to the square. People greet her on the way.

"How's it going, Auntie? How's your new puppy?"

"Fine, fine. Maurice is a good boy, a very good boy! Look! See how clean?" People look at him more closely. The Marais family? The Gilhoulacs? A woman hands him a walnut and then laughs with surprise at the quick, deft crack with which he shatters it on the cobbles, and his expertise at plucking the meat from the shells.

In the square the baker squats solemnly before the boy and gives him a roll, still oven-warm. The boy sniffs at it, turning it over twice before he hands it back. The baker feigns surprise and then offense.

"Potatoes!" the old woman explains proudly. "Jean-Claude will eat only baked potatoes, and they must be hot from the coals!"

It seems to her that the boy has always been there, though it's been just a week and, except for the outings, he's no trouble at all. But the outings exhaust her. Even now that he carries her loaded basket—and she makes sure never to go when the schoolboys are out—by the time she reaches her door after being dragged through the town and back up the hill, her feet are on fire and her legs and back are knotted with pain.

She shoves her door open and pulls the boy in. Wheezing, she takes the basket from him and sets it on the table.

She unties the rope from around her waist and then she has to sit, groaning for a moment, for the sake of her feet and back and heart.

In that moment the boy—Jean-Paul, Robert, Maurice, Henri—slips past her out the door. Beatrice blinks and sees the rope's end flip around the doorway and vanish. She throws herself out of the chair, stumbles to the door, and arrives at the sill on her knees. A tremendous hoarse wail comes up and out of her. Faces appear in windows all up and down the narrow street. They see the old woman in her doorway on her hands and knees, howling.

Far up the road to the mountain, they see a small, gowned figure moving very fast.

Berries! Wherever he goes there are berries because he only goes where the berries are. Anything that is not a berry is pushed aside and disappears. He wades through the thick, pulsing odor of juice simmering in the sun, plucking only the ripest and plumpest until he is as full and ripe as any berry.

Lids slide down his eyes, and he dreams he is plucking berries and eating berries, plucking potatoes and eating potatoes. The berries' sweet glow and the ashy savor of the potatoes melt into one warmth.

He wakes. He sees the moon and smells, or thinks he smells, the old woman—her hands, her hair, her dress. His palms reach out to touch her, and the sound that comes from his open mouth tries to touch her also. But she is not there.

He opens his eyes. Moonlight has thickened into a cool, soft fog. He moves through it, following a trail of woodsmoke that weaves between and around the pines. The smoke is joined and braided with dog and tobacco, wool and sweat. Soon, they form an enclosure of odors. He puts his head into it and sees fire.

"My God!"

The startled man chokes and coughs and sprays his family with soup and bread. His wife and children, even the nursing one, turn and simply stare. The frantic dog barks from under the table.

"My God!" says the man. "What the hell is it?" The boy stands in the doorway. The filthy shreds of what once might have been a shirt or gown hang from his neck. He doesn't look at the people or the dog. He ignores the barking, and he doesn't hear the man. His eyes and nose search the cabin's single room till he sees the basket. Running to it, he takes a potato in both hands. He flings it into the fire. Sparks and ashes fly up. The man stands abruptly, but his wife touches his arm.

"Look!" she whispers.

They all watch in silence as the boy, after a moment, reaches into the flames and retrieves the burning potato. He does not drop it or cry out in pain. He holds it, glowing, smoking, and blackened, in both hands, and devours it.

When it's gone, he trots out the door and disappears in the fog.

The man bursts into laughter.

"Was it a ghost, Papa?" His daughter wants to know. "Was it a demon?"

"No, no," says their mother. "It's just a poor crazy boy from the woods. From God."

He wandered north, following his nose, up the hills and mountains and across the high plateau. More and more frequently, he appeared in the doorways and streets of tiny villages. The hill people, farmers and shepherds, accepted him as he was. They let him come and go. Bread became food to him, and then carrots. These, and the smells of sweat and dogs and wool and burning wood, all became part of his world, and entered his dreams.

But the winter was as pitiless as the last had been, and even those who saw him more than once always shook their heads and crossed themselves in disbelief. Elfin and naked, except for a coat of snow, he appeared in their doorways and devoured potatoes that smoldered in his mouth. Then, refusing bed, coat, or blanket, he ran out into the drifts and blizzards and was swallowed up by the freezing darkness.

4

Constans-Saint-Estève, government commissioner for the town of Saint-Sernin in the Aveyron district of the south-central mountains of the Republic of France, dipped his pen and began his letter:

> *Saint-Sernin*
> *January 5, 1800*

"Damn!" he muttered, realizing his mistake. After six years, when he was excited, he *still* forgot! He crumpled the paper, tossed it to the floor, and on another sheet began again:

> *Saint-Sernin*
> *15 Nivôse, Year VIII*

Of all the idiocy, he paused to rage to himself, perpetrated by those murderous bastards that grabbed control of the Revolution—and almost took my head—the Republican calendar is as stupid as any! Time begins with the new Republic! *Poetic* months: Nivôse—snowy, Pluviôse—rainy, Ventôse—windy! Ten-day weeks! Maybe now that Bonaparte's taken over he'll get rid of this nonsense!

He shook his head, recalled his purpose:

To the President of the Administrative Board
Home for Orphaned Children
Town of Saint-Affrique

Citizen:

Something extraordinary has occurred: a child resembling a wild beast was captured this morning in the town square! A tanner named Vidal, looking out of his window at about 7 o'clock, saw a filthy child, between ten to fourteen years of age, digging in the snow around his garden. Although the weather was well below freezing, the child was completely naked. Vidal ran out shouting, but the child paid him no attention. When he tried to take hold of the boy, as he saw that was what it was, the child resisted fiercely and squirmed away. Vidal chased after him and called to his neighbors for help. Within a few seconds, a dozen citizens were chasing the boy through the streets. He was fast and agile, running sometimes upright and sometimes on all fours, dodging whoever tried to grab him. But finally, in the main square, they had him. He struggled, kicked, flailed, bit, and clawed, but did not get away.

He was brought to my office, where I found him squatting by the hearth rocking quickly back and forth before a blazing fire, which had his complete attention. When the crowd that filled the room pressed too close to him, he did not look at them but stirred uncomfortably and bared his teeth in a strange grimace. I approached him slowly and quietly so as not to alarm him further and began to speak softly to him, asking his name and so on. When he did not respond or react in any way, I spoke louder, with the same negative result, and it became clear to me that he was deaf. He allowed me to pat his head (his hair appears never to have been cut and is incredibly matted and filthy) and even to hug him gently and kiss his cheek. His eyes are bright, and his features fine and rather pretty.

Having won his confidence, I led him by the hand to my house and there offered him a great variety of foods, including cooked and raw meats, cheese, wheat and rye bread, apples, pears, grapes, parsnips, and potatoes. Ignoring all else, he seized two potatoes and hurled them into the fire. When they began to burn he snatched them out and, with every indication of pleasure and none of pain, he devoured them still glowing and smoking.

When I offered him wine, he pushed it away and drew me by the hand to a pitcher of water which he slapped repeatedly until I poured him a glass. He took it to the window and drank it avidly while looking out at the sky.

When he had finished, he handed me the empty glass and ran out the door and down the street toward the fields. I chased him for several minutes and it was all I could do to catch him. Once caught, he did not resist but seemed indifferent as I led him back to the house. He refused to stay in the bed I prepared for him, and slept instead on the floor beneath it.

Everything about this fascinating child gives the impression of a captured wild animal; it seems clear to me that he has lived in the wild from earliest childhood. I am informing the government, and would not be surprised if they put him into the hands of the brilliant Abbé Sicard, who has worked such wonders teaching the unfortunates at his Institute for Deaf-Mutes.

In the meantime I know you will provide him with the best of care, and allow me to emphasize that all precaution must be taken to prevent his escape. Although he seems quite content in captivity and obviously trusts me, his most constant passion, after food, is for freedom.

Greetings and regards,

Constans-Saint-Estève

5

In the vast courtyard of the Institute for Deaf-Mutes, everyone stands waiting. The students are arranged in ranks tended by their teachers. The maintenance staff is off to one side, and Julie stands close to her mother in the front row. She squeezes her mother's hand. Across the glare of the cobbles, in the shade of the ancient towering elm, stands a short, square, big-bellied man with a red face, Abbé Sicard. The *great* Abbé Sicard, head of the Institute, who, as her parents never tire of telling her, rescued the deaf and mute from asylums where they'd been abandoned with lunatics and idiots, and, with his genius and new methods of instruction, had transformed them into beings who not only could communicate their needs and desires but could reason and understand the meanings of hope, justice, and gratitude—and even the existence of God. The two times Julie has encountered him, he chucked her roughly under the chin with the damp, plump, snuff-scented fingers now clasped behind his back. He chats with the small group of men surrounding him, and nods frequently. They all watch the main gate.

For weeks now, on the street, in the shops and markets, all the talk has been of the wild boy captured in the south—someplace called Aveyron—who is being brought to Paris. And of all the places in Paris, it's coming *here*! Today . . . any minute now! The gazettes and journals are full of it, and people speak of nothing else. There is even a vaudeville song about it that her father sings and chuckles over:

> *. . . he lived up in a tree,*
> *knew nothing of Liberty!*
> *And so we had to capture him,*
> *to tell him he was free,*
> *a Revolutionary citizen,*
> *just like you and me!*

Her father once saw some savages from America, all painted red and dressed in feathers. He says this one is even more savage; barely human, it wears nothing and eats live birds. He so wanted to see it, but his chest has him in bed again. I must be the only person in the world, she thinks, who doesn't care to see the creature. She has even had dreams about it—awful ones she can't quite remember. But because of it, and the kindness of the Abbé Sicard, she and her sisters were able to leave off their sewing—the endless seams, the myriad buttonholes—and here she is on a weekday, holding her mother's hand.

Her mother is a cook in the vast kitchens and her father cares for the vegetable gardens, and usually it's only Sundays that Julie can be with them. They live at the Institute, but girls are not allowed to live here—too disruptive, says Abbé Sicard. So Julie must live with her sisters, Rose and Evelyn, and Evelyn's husband, Nicholas. Julie smiles to herself. Nicholas is such fun! He had read them the news accounts of the wild boy while they were sewing, and then leaped around the kitchen just like a monkey; she thought she'd fall off her chair from laughing. He's so funny. And he likes me. If only he wouldn't . . .

Julie will be eleven in Frimaire. Rose is seventeen and Evelyn is twenty and has a new baby. Albert. She hears her sisters behind her, whispering and fussing over him. He was named after their little brother, Albert, who died when Julie was six. All Julie's other brothers died before she was born, so everyone is mad for little Albert, especially Julie's mother, who thinks girls don't matter, only boys. To Julie, Albert's mostly a nuisance—someone else who needs taking care of—though she'd rather take care of him than sew. She and her sisters do out-work at home and little Albert likes to scream while they're sewing. The worst are buttonholes. Julie often dreams that she's sewing—on and on through the night—which makes sleep as tedious as work. Hunched over a piece of cloth and a needle day after day, she feels sometimes that she has died.

There's shuffling and squirming to her right, near the door of the main building. Again and again, with gestures, pinches, and slaps, teachers warn the students, all deaf, they must be still, but from the corners of her eyes Julie glimpses sly hands flashing provocative messages and faces near bursting with suppressed excitement and hilarity. Two straight-faced boys furtively argue with vehement signs. One claims the savage has a long furry tail. The other signs that the first is crazy, and then, noticing that Julie is watching them, he elbows his friend. They grimace and wriggle their fingers at her. She quickly looks away.

When Julie first visited here, the deaf boys seemed grotesque and frightening. They would stare at her silently, or grunt and squeal, making elaborate gyrations. They seemed barely human. But now she sees how their fingers, bodies, and faces weave words and pictures—words she can almost hear and pictures she can almost see. Their every conversation is like a vaudeville show. Sometimes she envies their exuberance and community and wonders if she could learn their language. But she is still afraid.

There is shouting from the streets, and a man runs in and warns that the carriage is just a couple of blocks away. The atmosphere of excitement swells.

The cheers and shouts are louder now and Julie can hear the horses' hooves on the cobbles, the rattle of the carriage.

Everything changes; mountains become hills, hills become fields and vineyards; villages come and go; several cities watch them pass. Inside the carriage, the boy huddled on the floor, rocking and rocked by its bouncing, does not see them. There is nothing to see. He embraces a rough, lumpy sack. All that matters is within the sack. *His* sack. He has become an *owner* of *things.* Things that may be lost or taken away; ownership is a fragile state. The sack contains all that can be put into a sack of what he knows and cares for: potatoes, baked and raw, green walnuts, chestnuts, acorns, and handfuls of dried broad beans in their crackling pods. The rocky hills, mountainsides of bramble and oak, the rivers of boulders, those are left behind.

He sleeps and dreams sometimes, but dreaming and waking are the same to him, rocked by the carriage as he rocks his bag and rocks himself. Endlessly.

He has a vague awareness that the thudding sound of hooves has become a clattering on stone that is soon tangled with the syncopated clatter of other hooves and the rattle of other carriages; rattling and clattering that multiplies, then doubles, is punctuated with shouts and barking, and doubles again, like echoes echoing echoes, each becoming louder. The smells, too, reproduce themselves: horse sweat, horse dung, horse urine. The vapors fill the carriage like a thick, hot soup and his eyes water. Other odors float or swim in it. There are pockets and flashes of human sweat, sweet and sour; occasional waves of warm, yeasty bread; a river of sweet-salt blood and then pungent sausage. His nostrils flutter, and saliva escapes the corners of his mouth. Here and there, in cool splashes, the scent of trees in full leaf spills over him. A sudden banging on the sides of the racketing carriage. Shrill cries. Small grimy fingers appear, clutching at the open windowsills, followed by filthy, snot-nosed faces with staring eyes and open mouths. On the boy's neck, tiny hairs bristle.

"Get off! Get off!" the two men on the seats shout. They slap at the tenacious fingers, and the protesting faces drop away. But they bob alongside, and some hang on to the back and try to see in. The boy stares at the floor and shifts uneasily. He clutches his bag and bares his teeth.

The rocking stops. The clattering stops. Everything stops, and from outside, smells of sweat and cologne, wine and garlic, powder and tobacco—the smells of people—triumph over the smells of horse. The carriage door swings open, and, pushed from behind, pulled from in front, the boy tumbles out into Paris.

A wave of signs ripples through the expectant courtyard and Julie feels her mother's hand tighten. Now there is a silence from the street, like a great intake of breath.

"Oh my God!" She hears a woman's voice. Then a man's.

"Look at this!"

"Amazing!"

Two men come through the gate; one is fat and important looking, the other older and more rustic. Between them trots a small, dark-haired boy of about Julie's age. He is immediately repellent to her. A rope tied round his waist is held by the older man. The boy wears what looks like a gray nightshirt and hugs a big lumpy brown sack. He takes quick little steps that rock him from side to side, and it's clear that if not for the rope, which holds him back like a pony's reins, his trot would be a gallop. If he has a tail, the gown hides it.

The three walk up to the Abbé Sicard and the other notables under the tree. The men shake hands, and then Sicard extends his hand to the boy, who leans forward and, like a puppy, sniffs it all over. Gasps are heard, and scattered squeals and grunts from the students, but the startled director quickly recovers himself. He smiles broadly and pats the boy's head. Then he turns to the students and teachers lined up behind him, and with grand, sweeping waves of his hands, which he uses to sign, and a big, resounding voice, he speaks:

"In this new age of the Republic and the 'rights of man,' there are many urgent questions to which this poor creature—this boy—might offer us the key: What is man's true nature before it is improved or distorted by society? What is God-given and what is learned? How do we become what we are, and what might we, under other circumstances, become? After he is carefully examined by a committee of our finest scientific minds, members of the Society of Observers of Man, with hopes of learning something of man's true and rudimentary nature, you may rest assured that this innocent child of the forest will soon— with skill, patience, and love—be indistinguishable from you others here: you students in your blue velour, your faces radiating intelligence, reason, and faith in the supreme intelligence that rules us all . . ."

The students double over squealing and some dance in little circles, and several of the teachers laugh out loud, even as they clamp hands over their mouths and turn away. Sicard is astonished. He glances down at the boy who squats beside him, and, just in time to save his shoes, he hops away from the stream of liquid that pours from under the gray linen gown. It snakes across the flagstones and Sicard's face reddens. He admonishes the students, reminding them that this poor unfortunate has not yet had their advantages, without which, he declares in clear signs, they might be squatting there as abjectly and innocently as he.

This thought sets the children off again, and without further ceremony Sicard leads the visitors in Julie's direction on their way to the broad front staircase of the main building.

As they pass close, her mother, having imagined just this opportunity, holds out a handful of roasted chestnuts. Julie shrinks back. My God! she thinks, why is she doing this? The boy snuffles at her mother's hand; it sounds exactly like a dog. He snatches the chestnuts so quickly they seem to vanish, and then looks into her hand, rather than her face, for more.

"Hello . . . hello, my sweet . . ." her mother whispers, and caresses the boy's cheek. His eyes never rest but flit continually over everything and everyone with equal disinterest like some animal's in the zoo. Julie stares at him. From inches away, his gaze slides like a snake, over, around, and through her and she shudders—a sensation of being touched and of being invisible. What if he got loose?

"Don't be afraid," says the older man, holding the boy's

rope. "He's really a very good boy." He smiles at Julie and rubs the boy's head. "Yes, a very good boy," he croons as he leads him up the stairs, ". . . very, very good." They disappear into the Institute.

Inside. The sun is gone. The sky is gone. There is no food here. He clutches his sack. Stone is everywhere. He smells dead water and the creeping fungus that loves the dark. He smells great distances, all of stone, all damp and silent. He's led up a hill of stone. These are stairs. Here are more stairs. This is a hall, all of stone, like a tunnel of stone. Along the way, large, silent eyes peer and mouths grimace and hands and fingers flap and flutter. The tiny hairs on the back of his neck tell him to run, but he can't run. His belly spasms. This is a door. Sometimes doors offer release. Sometimes behind them there is outside. But not this door. This is your room. There is your bed. These are your toys. This is your chamber pot. Do you know what a chamber pot is? He runs to the window. He presses his face against the pane and slaps at it with his palms. He tries to smell the light. He sees trees, woods, sky, and clouds. But all he can smell or feel is glass.

Come. Come over here and see your bed. This is your bed. He sniffs at dead grass wrapped in a gown, as he is wrapped in a gown. This is something he knows. He crawls onto it and wriggles backward, till he can go no farther. Against the stone he feels, vibrating through it, a wave of shuffling and clumping, coming closer and closer, pushing ahead of it a hint of breeze scented with tobacco and sweat.

41

The door opens and the room fills with broadcloth, silk and velvet, starch, white linen, cologne, and more sweat. A hand emerges and gives him the sun. Its smell is harsh and strange. This is an orange. Have you had an orange before? He gives it back. He looks up at all the moist, blinking eyes. They surround him and come closer, and a murmurous babble of voices rises like a wall.

6

Abbé Sicard, as he pushed his way through the crowd and into the room, heard a woman scream. "He tried to bite me! Let me out!" He couldn't see her, but her voice shrilled above the others.

"Excuse me!" boomed Sicard. "Let us through!" He pushed irresistibly forward like a small wall, with a pale, dark-suited young man shuffling close in his wake.

"Let us through! Let us through!" But he couldn't hear his own words above the babble, and increasing pressure from inside held him back momentarily.

"Look! Here, see the teeth marks?" wailed the woman's voice.

"Let us out!" A man's voice, and then another, joined hers. "Let us out! I'm going to demand our money back!" The young man, forced up against Sicard's back, groaned.

"Is it always like this?" he shouted in the abbé's ear.

"This is unusual," grunted the abbé, pushing ahead. They heard a high-pitched bird-like shrieking, rising and falling, and then, "Look out! Look what he's doing! Get back!"

The abbé glimpsed a woman's pale face flanked by two shouting men moving toward the door; their outward surge allowed him to lunge into the room. "Let me through!" he bellowed. "I'm the director! Let me through!" A man in front of him looked around and squeezed aside.

"I'm the director and I have a doctor here! Let me through!"

An aisle opened and the abbé and the doctor saw the gowned boy—teeth bared, eyes rolling—standing on the bed and shrieking. He flailed his arms and then spun around and hurled himself at the wall, clawed it, and tried to bite it. They reached him as he fell back on the bed and attacked the mattress. His shrieks became bleats. He revolved round and round, trying to wrap himself in a blanket. As the doctor knelt by the bed, the boy stopped suddenly, arched his back, and went rigid. His eyes showed only a thin quivering crescent of pupil above the whites. His head began whipping from side to side; foam flecked his lips and flew from his mouth.

"Does this happen often?" the doctor asked Sicard.

"Not this," said the director, leaning closer and shaking his head. "Not this!"

"It's all right now," the doctor intoned softly close to the boy's ear. "Calm now, calm . . ." He took the boy's hand. "It's all right." The crowd leaned over them to hear.

"Please!" The abbé hissed, snapping his head around.

"Give him air! Let him be!" Startled, they moved back and watched the young man—hawk-like in his attention and profile—soothe the writhing child. The gurgles and moans from the boy began to subside.

"Everyone! It's time to leave!" Sicard turned on the crowd. "The viewing is over. Out, please! Out!" Arms spread, he herded them toward the door.

"This creature attacked a woman here today," said a tall, balding man. "I write for the *Journal*. When will we have your committee's report, Abbé? It's been weeks now. Is this a savage, or a hoax, or what?"

"Soon, soon." Sicard bellied him firmly backward. "We of the Society of Observers of Man are examining and testing him most thoroughly. Soon we will publish our findings. Until then, the public viewings are discontinued. They've clearly become disturbing to the child. It's become a circus! Soon you'll know everything. Good day, sir."

The short, square abbé looked as if he could walk through a wall if he so decided. And indeed, since surviving Fructidorization—the term used for the fate of the victims of the massacres of Fructidor, year I—he seemed to fear nothing. He was one of the churchmen who had refused to swear allegiance to the Revolution, and was dragged from his classroom at sword point and condemned to death by the Committee for Executions. He was loaded, with five other priests, into an open carriage and driven through streets lined with sword-thrusting citizens. Slashed repeatedly and dripping with blood, they arrived at the execution courtyard, where the executioner was a mob of "citizens" armed with axes, knives, and scythes. One at a time, the priests were pulled from the carriage and carved to pieces. Sicard, crouching on the floor under a pile of pillows, was somehow overlooked, and when a second coachful of prisoners arrived and was mobbed, he ran into a government building, burst into a committee meeting, and pleaded with them to save him. The armed mob discovered his absence and burst in after him. "There's the son of a bitch! Skewer him!" Sicard leaped up onto a mantelpiece and bellowed, "I instruct the deaf and mute! The children of the poor! Your children! I work for you!"

"It's the Abbé Sicard!" shouted one of the mob. "The father of the deaf-mutes! Spare him!" The cry was taken up, "Spare him!" His executioners now wanted to carry him home, triumphant. Sicard could hear the pleading and screams of his colleagues in the courtyard; he insisted on being held until he was released officially. Locked in a closet, he spent the entire night hearing the choirs of screams, near and far, that floated over the city. In the morning, when he was released, Sicard tottered out, stepping carefully over severed arms and legs. Corpses filled the courtyards of Paris. Gutters ran with blood.

He returned to the Institute, where his growing renown seemed to encourage his bullheadedness; he continued to publish pro-Catholic and anti-Revolutionary pamphlets, and had only recently emerged from two years in exile, pardoned—thanks to the pleas of his grateful students—by Napoléon Bonaparte, who had no love for him.

Having survived all this, he was now believed to be indestructible as well as infallible. Yes, he continued to work wonders with the deaf, but what the hell was he supposed to do with this, this *creature* they had sent him? He looked down at the pale, filth-smeared child twitching fitfully on the stained mattress, and shook his head.

"Is it epilepsy?" Sicard asked the doctor.

"It may be." The young man held the boy's hand, stared into his eyes, and patted his forehead with a handkerchief. "But it could just as well be the crowds." He looked up at the abbé. "I might react the same way."

"Well," said the abbé, "that's the end of it. Only I and the other Society members will have access to him." The boy, lying on his back, was rocking now, from side to side, and humming a two-note tune over and over. He stared at the ceiling as if watching something there.

"What *have* you learned about him?" asked the doctor, still watching the boy intently.

Sicard grunted a wry chuckle and shrugged. "Except for his origins—nobody's come to claim him—there seems to be little to learn. I tried bells, shouts, trumpets. I fired a pistol just next to his ear; he didn't blink. Totally deaf, right? Then someone cracks a walnut in the next room and instantly the boy climbs over us to reach it. He responds to nothing but food. Nothing. He can pick up burning potatoes—in *flames*, mind you—and devour them with no sign of pain. He's marvelously dextrous, can move his fingers in any direction and pick up the tiniest objects—if they interest him. He's able to run with a full pan of water without spilling a drop. In studying him one feels invisible, because he seems absolutely unaware that anyone else exists unless they bring food or tickle him. Oh yes, he loves to be tickled under his chin—right where someone put that nasty scar—he'll take your hand and put it there to show what he wants. Before coming here he was observed for six months in the south by a naturalist named Bonnaterre. Evidently the man became quite fond of him, said the boy had an 'inexplicable charm,' which I have yet to see. During that time, according to the man's report, the child learned to shell and sort dried beans, tossing away the bad ones and allowing no good one to escape. He also discovered he could use the pods to fuel the cooking fire. He would bury any food left over from a meal in little caches around the yard, and he never forgot where any of them were. He insists the child even learned to use a chamber pot, but here, more often than not, he forgets the pot and uses his bed— or anywhere he happens to be. If this is the primal nature of man, well, it's very disappointing. I'm forced to believe it's idiocy, pure and simple."

The doctor studied the boy, and the abbé studied the doctor and his remarkable expression of attention—the result, it seemed, of dark, deep-set eyes peering out from under a vast forehead guarded by an eagle of a nose. His name was Itard, and he had come to the Institute this morning, running up the street from Val-de-Grâce, the army hospital, in response to a call for a doctor to set a student's broken leg. He obviously knew his business, and Sicard had liked him immediately. When asked if he had any interest in seeing the "wild boy," he had responded enthusiastically.

"Has he suffered from catarrh—sneezing? Coughing?"

"No," said the abbé. "Couldn't get him to sneeze even with his nose full of snuff!" The child now lay on his side hugging his knees, rocking gently back and forth, eyes closed, his breathing more normal.

"He's quiet now," said Sicard. "Let's let him rest." They went out into the hall, and Sicard closed and locked the door behind them. The shrieks began immediately. The door shook when the boy's body hit it; then it jerked and rattled, and they heard clawing on the wood. The young man, obviously dismayed, was startled, and turned a shade paler.

"This is *normal*," the abbé assured him, putting an arm around his shoulders. "He does this every time we lock his door. But tell me, Citizen Itard—since we have no doctor here, would you consider being the boy's physician? It would be a matter of looking in on him every few days. I'm afraid we couldn't pay much . . ."

The young man turned to the abbé. His eyes looked out past his jutting nose and overhung brow like two small animals peering from a cave. The abbé saw surprise, doubt, and then, slowly, a glowing warmth.

"I would be delighted," said the doctor. He added a curt nod and a tiny, tight-lipped smile. "But . . . may I ask one more question?"

"Of course."

"Have you ever seen the child weep?"

Sicard thought for a moment.

"Never," he said.

7

8 *Frimaire, Year IX*
(November 29, 1800)

Jean-Marc-Gaspard Itard sat quietly in the middle of the lecture hall. Around him the members of the Society of Observers of Man greeted colleagues and searched for seats, and, unnoticed, he watched them. He studied faces, clothes, and gestures and caught snatches of gossip, political and professional, as well as speculations on the report that was about to be delivered: "On the Boy Known as the Savage of Aveyron."

The only two members he knew, aside from Sicard, had been his teachers and were on the platform as part of the committee. He knew what their conclusions were; Sicard had told him. And in spite of them, he had made his decision. There was a trembling in his belly and his pulse was quick. He was poised, as if for a great leap that would render him visible to these exceptional citizens for whom he did not yet exist.

What he did not know were all the findings and arguments that had led to the committee's conclusions. The final report had been written by his teacher, Pinel, medical director of Bicêtre, the asylum for the insane. The great Pinel. Might Pinel's thinking cause him to change his mind? To abandon his plan? Of course it might, and the pain of this possibility—the disappointment—made him wince every time it came to mind. But he must be objective; he must refute Pinel on Pinel's terms.

The committee members sat at ease on the platform: Sicard, his square face ruddy—the savior of the deaf in his ribbons and medals; Jauffret, the naturalist, tall, lean, and, even in his wig, looking wind-blown; the skeletal Cuvier, with whom Itard had studied anatomy; the Baron De Gerando, at only twenty-eight—two years older than Itard—this former simple soldier with the sleek, pleasant look of a seal was now a noted philosopher and statesman. Sicard was introducing Pinel. The hall fell quiet and Pinel cleared his throat.

How many hours had Itard spent gazing into this precisely featured face beneath its towering forehead, noting each word produced by that mouth with its slight, wry smile? Just eight years before, Pinel had done for the insane what Sicard had done for the deaf; he had unlocked the dungeons and chains of the vast Bicêtre madhouse and declared the inmates to be citizens who were not bewitched but simply ill. He had clothed them, bathed them, fed them, and allowed them out into the light and air, and in all of them, madness had diminished, and in many, it vanished completely. Then he'd gone about defining, naming, and categorizing the illnesses from which they suffered, and began to look for causes and cures. The great Pinel.

"For many weeks now," he began, "my colleagues and I have studied, from the points of view of our various disciplines, the child known as the Savage of Aveyron, who was found in the mountainous southern wilds of the Republic. Because of his appearance and primitive behavior, many believed the child to be completely uncontaminated by society, and thus presenting an opportunity to study human nature in its purest form, undistorted by any kind of education or social interaction. Unfortunately, what we found was a child of extremely low intelligence, totally incapable of speaking or of ever learning to speak, and offering nothing that could possibly contribute to our knowledge of human nature."

At every pause, Itard found himself holding his breath. The report was lengthy and detailed. It went on to describe the boy's appearance, demeanor, and behavior and to compare him to children and adults whom Pinel himself had diagnosed as idiots, a class of mental defective beyond any hope of cure, training, or improvement. It was to this category he belonged rather than to any known class of savage. Even when measured against the intelligence and behavior of certain animals, the boy was obviously inferior. His total lack of response to music placed his sensibility below that of the elephant, as well as that of many idiots, and even his acute sense of smell—obviously sharpened by his life in the wild—did not keep him from defecating in his bed, something no wild or domestic animal would ever do. He had no interest in, and would not even look at, anything he could not eat or use for escape; a beautifully carved cameo, after a glance, left him cold. He studied his reflection in a mirror, but so did cats and monkeys, and unlike them, he could not distinguish between a real object and its reflected or painted image. He could hear, but responded only to sounds relating to his immediate needs—the sound of water being poured, the threat of a barking dog . . .

Some of the things that this fellow, Bonnaterre, had pointed out in his earlier report—such as the child having learned to cook his own food—were obviously the result of ape-like imitation motivated by physical need. The cutting of bread, for example, was beyond him, and he would eat meat, cooked or raw, indiscriminately.

His occasional outbursts of laughter were the same as those heard in asylums and, rather than the result of some amusing memory, came from an absence of ideas. His slight smile when receiving some kindness was the merest shadow of true feeling. His condition, rather than the result of his being abandoned in the wild, was obviously the cause of it. His ability to survive was due only to the most basic instincts rather than any kind of intelligence.

"Does not all the evidence tell us that this so-called Savage of Aveyron is to be considered in that category of people I have classified as idiots? Now, what are the usual causes of idiocy in childhood? They are basically three: a mother who becomes terrified while giving birth to her child; an infant suffering convulsions due to some sort of infection or intense fright; or teething that is extremely painful and difficult. Whichever one of these three produced this state in our subject—and we cannot know for certain—he was clearly then abandoned, perhaps by depraved, poverty-stricken parents who botched an attempt to end his life by slashing his throat. Driven by hunger and animal instinct, the child foraged, devouring whatever he could find, and, possessed of a strong constitution and sheer good fortune, he managed to survive until he was captured and brought to us. His intellect, such as it is, played no part in it.

"What, then, must our conclusions be? In short, that he is simply an idiot and, like all idiots, hopeless."

Itard sat still while, around him, questions were asked and clarifications requested. His breath short, his pulse pounding, he was at the verge of standing and shouting, "You have missed the essential here! You are wrong!" but was held in his seat by the voice of reason—of his father—that intoned in his ear, "Who do you think you are? Who are you to question the great Pinel?"

8

Sundays are so brief, thinks Julie, so precious—why must we ruin them doing this? Carrying a basket of bread and nuts, she follows her mother up the stairs to the third floor of the Institute. Her mother has towels, soap, a pitcher of hot water, and a basin. At the dark end of a long hall they stop. Madame Guérin taps gently at a door.

"Hello? Hello? May we come in, please?" There is no answer. Madame Guérin tries her key but the door is unlocked.

Julie gags. Beside the torn, filthy mattress the overflowing chamber pot buzzes with flies. More flies batter and rage at the single window, and countless lifeless others litter the sill and floor beneath it. The room is strewn with dust-covered toys, each where she'd seen it the week before and the weeks before that. A doll with blond ringlets sprawls grinning at the ceiling, its blue silk dress smeared with filth. A carriage with doors that open and close lies on its side along with its matched team. With her toe, Julie touches a music box. A ballerina in a gauzy gown balances on top.

"I will never have such things," she says to herself each time she sees them. "I will never have them . . ."

The boy is not there.

"Oh dear, oh dear!" Her mother sighs. "We'll look up in the attic. That's where he usually hides. Bring the basket!"

She leaves the pitcher by the door and hurries down the hall. Julie runs after.

"It's shameful!" her mother hisses as she searches the rooms they pass. "Shameful! They take better care of the cats and dogs! I can't get up here all the time, and when I do I can't find him. They bring him all the way to Paris, as if he's some kind of scientific miracle. They make a big fuss, and suddenly, 'Oh! He's just an idiot!' and they toss him aside like trash! He's a boy! He's a baby! What did they think he was? Now the gawkers don't come, the boys chase him and torment him—wouldn't you hide? It shows intelligence! I thought they brought him here to help him, to teach him. But no! They don't even wash him. He's gotten worse. Much worse! Bicêtre! That's where they say they're going to send him. Do you know what it's like, Bicêtre?"

Please, prays Julie as they hurry up the stairs, please send him to Bicêtre. Madame Guérin stops two boys with her upraised hand. She does a little dance meant to be the savage's walk, then raises her eyebrows and shrugs. The boys grin. They make squeaks that Julie knows are giggles, then shake their heads and gallop on down the stairs. On the top floor a toothless old man, Antoine the caretaker, nods emphatically when he sees them, and pumps a finger at the ceiling. Julie's heart sinks even lower: the attic. She follows her mother up a ladder into the dusty, cobwebbed gloom.

Stepping carefully, she pursues her mother's shape and sounds down aisles of broken and forgotten things. She knows there are rats here. She can smell them. Her mother calls softly, then stops to listen. Julie hears the savage's squeaky, monotonous moan. They move toward it into darkness, zigzagging between piles of scrap lumber and chunks of plaster. The boy has wedged himself between stacks of broken shingles, and Julie can just make out his eyes. She stays back as her mother stoops and, murmuring softly, works her way close. Now Julie can see neither of them, and she stands alone in the rat-musty dark. She stands there for what seems an endless time before her mother says, "Give me the food, and go get the water and towels."

Julie finds the pitcher and basin where she left them. She's startled when a man comes out of the savage's room. His nose seems enormous and his eyes very dark. He wears a black suit and white ruffled shirt. He studies her a moment before he asks if she knows where the savage might be. When she answers, he tells her to leave the pitcher and basin and to show him the way.

In the attic he kneels beside her mother. They exchange whispered words, her mother's fervent. Julie waits, hoping they leave the boy where he is, but finally, with her mother and the man each holding an arm, they coax him out of his nest. They have to lift him down the ladder. He's covered with dirt and cobwebs, and he looks much smaller than when she saw him last. His eyes are screwed shut, as if he's still hiding.

They lead him slowly down the stairs and toward his room. He moves hesitantly until he hears a swarm of squeals and footsteps, and tries to run. Her mother and the man hold him close between them as they're surrounded by wide-eyed, gesticulating boys. The savage's teeth are bared, his eyes wide and quivering. The man waves the boys away and they back off down the hall as he strokes the child's head to calm him. In his room, the child scuttles like a cockroach into a corner. By the gray light from the fly-spattered window he looks like a pile of dirty rags, rocking.

Julie notices the room brightening. The sun, hidden all morning behind thick clouds, is working itself free. Silver light floods the room and the boy's eyes flash and come alive. He laughs and his laugh, gleeful like a baby's, takes them by surprise. His smile seems pure joy. He reaches his hands toward the window as the light begins to slip away. The room darkens and Julie sees his face and eyes cloud over till he's exactly as before. They stand in silence staring at him. His soul, thinks Julie, is hidden by clouds.

Her mother turns to her.

"Julie," she says, "this is Dr. Itard. Doctor, this is my youngest."

Julie curtsies and says, "Sir." Above his distracting nose and pale brow, the man's hair is brown and curly. His eyes are very serious. They look directly into hers. He takes her hand and repeats her name.

"What will become of him now?" she asks, pointing her chin at the savage.

The doctor looks at her thoughtfully before he answers.

"Just this morning," he says at last, "Abbé Sicard put the child completely into my care. First, I will feed and bathe him. I will show him that we care for him, and that he has a place here. And then, I will help him to understand that he is a person—a human being—just like you."

Julie sees that her mother is smiling.

9

11 Nivôse, Year IX
(January 1, 1801)

Itard sits on a cold, damp bench of stone in the gray garden. Through the icy drizzle, he looks across the lily pond. The shriveled pads are black and frozen. He watches the boy.

This excitement I feel—this joy—reminds me of when I was given my first puppy. He's mine!

But who is he? Who is this boy?

When they first came out, hours ago, the child's eyes opened wide. With a shriek of joyous laughter he ran in circles through the desolate flower beds. Exactly like an ecstatic puppy, thinks Itard—except for the laughter. Puppies don't laugh; *children* laugh. Even idiot children.

Barefoot and wearing only a linen nightshirt, the boy is everywhere at once. He chases wind-blown leaves and tumbles with them over the paths and into hedges. Occasional flurries of snow cause pure delirium. And whenever the wind blows a sudden gust, he whoops and whirls into the air, and the doctor laughs. How long since I've laughed like this? he wonders. It's as if I remember myself running naked through the rain in a wintry garden. Have I ever done that? As a child at home? Never. And yet . . .

Home. Hills in sight of mountains, maybe not too different from the ones this boy knew. After eight years away, four of them in Paris, the word "home" was still pungent with smells: his mother's kitchen; his father's workshop . . . pine shavings, the simmering glue pot. His father watching him. His father is still there in the tiny village, but Jean-Marc-Gaspard is here. Here in Paris, a doctor! When he was in school, his passions had been philosophy, science, and the church. If it hadn't been for the Revolution, he would have become a lay priest—like his uncle, the canon—to teach and study. His father had wanted him in business. His father would have had him in a Marseilles bank, scratching inky figures into endless ledgers, if the war hadn't saved him. "The Republic requires that all male citizens between the ages of eighteen and thirty take up arms in its defense . . ." His father wrote to a family friend who pulled some strings, and almost overnight, at the age of nineteen, with no training, Itard was an army health officer in a hospital, bandaging and rebandaging the oozing stumps of the groaning men who surrounded him.

He had never dreamed of becoming a doctor, but he felt surprisingly at home; the gore didn't bother him. He repaired the men with an expertise he'd learned from his father, repairing chairs and bureau drawers. The revealed secrets of the body fascinated him. He learned quickly and was transferred to the port of Toulon, after Napoléon Bonaparte, a twenty-four-year-old general, had taken it back from the counter-revolutionaries and their British allies. Here, Itard's real education began. The Republican army was in the process of punishing the town for its betrayal of the Revolution, and Itard learned of human cruelty, seeing men do things to other men—and to women—that he could never have imagined: images that still flashed unexpectedly through his mind and made him wince and grit his teeth, horrors that still crawled into his dreams. But it was also here that he met Dr. Larrey, his first great teacher of medicine. Larrey had liked him; these great men, older men, they seemed to like him. It always surprised him. Was it his astute questions? His quiet enthusiasm? He felt so inarticulate, so chaotic in his thinking—but they liked him.

Three years later, Itard was sent as a doctor to Val-de-Grâce, the great military hospital in the heart of Paris. Here he could practice medicine, and study with the greatest practitioners of the day. Paris! The center of the world. A young man's world! Anything is possible, all doors are open. In a political coup, Bonaparte, now thirty, became the ruler of France; De Gerando, an anonymous soldier, wrote a philosophic essay and won instant fame and a place in the new government; and Itard, by the fluke of a deaf child falling down a flight of stairs, was now *here*—in the Institute garden—in charge of this boy. He's mine.

Itard stands, blows on his fingers, and trots after the child. From time to time, he tries to engage him in play—

tag, hide-and-seek—but the boy is given over to the leaves, wind, and sleet.

There were idiot children in our village. They never made me laugh. I've seen the children at Bicêtre smeared with feces. When I look at this one, I see something else. What do I see? Do I know better than Pinel what an idiot is? Or what causes idiocy? But why not a defect in the blood? A flaw in the egg? The sperm? A shock in the womb? An infant dropped on its head?

Or abandonment. Why not abandonment? A fourteen-year-old peasant girl impregnated in the cow barn by an uncle gives birth squatting in the woods and leaves the infant along with the placenta under the brambles . . . No. To have survived, he must have been older. If, at the age of three—or even four—I had been abandoned by my parents (incredible thought! My righteous father, my sickly saintly mother) after one of them had tried to cut my throat (Mother? Never! She so hates mess and blood. Father? Maybe, if he believed, like Abraham, that God required it. Then, a master carpenter, he'd have done a perfect job. Maybe—Itard chuckled at the thought—the two together: Mother holding me and looking away, Father with the knife . . .), or maybe if, like Oedipus, I was given to a servant who botched the killing, or hadn't the heart, and then left me in the woods, what would I do? Wander crying, calling for help?

Would I call? If my own parents—my flesh and my blood, my sole shelter and security in this cruel world—

had turned on me . . . who, then, could I expect to help me? Would I expect help at all? Wouldn't I crawl, hardly daring to breathe, to hide myself in bushes or brambles, under fallen trees? And if I heard or saw anything human, I'd cover myself with earth and leaves, or run the other way, till only woods and wilderness surrounded me. And then I'd pray they'd never find me. And having run and hid and crawled, exhausted by fear, I'd curl up between the mossy roots of some great tree and sleep. Blessed sleep. Waking in the night, terrified, hearing owls and wolves, and remembering that I was completely alone, I would weep—but silently—deep, deep inside myself. At dawn, hunger would wake me, rouse me out of my nest, and I'd wander, with hunger a constant ache. I would taste this and chew on that. I'd find nuts, acorns, wild onions . . . Coming upon berries, I'd gorge myself. And as the days passed, my parents, my home, would begin to seem a dream that, blessedly, recedes and fades at the same time the trunks and roots of certain trees become as familiar as the legs of my mother's furniture had been. And after days and weeks of rain and months of snow, after winters of hunger, after years of not speaking or hearing speech, forgetting words and people and even how to weep, years of endless foraging in woods that have become, for me, home and mother and father—I would be this boy.

Itard is shivering. He blows on his fingers and rubs his hands together. The boy rolls and splashes in half-frozen puddles. Pinel says he's hopeless . . . and Sicard, Cuvier, the others. These great minds—my teachers, so much older, more experienced and learned than I. How could they miss what I see so clearly? What will they say if I have the boy speak to them?

The afternoon darkens and the boy's pace slows. He trots round and round the lily pond and finally settles beside it and rocks himself. His face twitches and he moans his endless song. An hour passes as Itard watches. The rocking slows. The boy's wet gown flaps in the icy wind, but his face and body become still. He looks into the pond. His eyes reflect the water that reflects the darkening sky.

And then, slowly, he picks up a handful of dead leaves and lets them fall, gently, one by one, to the surface of the pond. He watches as they drift away. His eyes have become as black and deep as the pond. And for a long while, he's absolutely still.

The doctor catches himself not breathing. He exhales and an immense wave of pain, grief, and joy floods through him. Who am I looking at? Are you myself? Who are you?

The doctor wipes his eyes. This boy, he thinks, is the center and sole occupant of his own world. How can we know who or what we are except in relation . . . in society? We'll begin at this beginning.

He pulls a notebook from his pocket, a new one, specially purchased, and rummages for the pencil. His thoughts race each other, become tangled and jumbled; writing, making notes, he had found, helped.

1. Waken the boy to society.

My God, what does he know of it, except being imprisoned and gawked at, examined and prodded by doctors, and tormented by other children. All he cares for is eating and running wild. Good! I'll give him all he wants, but as much as possible, I'll make them social activities.

2. Awaken his senses.
a. Touch.

He knows neither hot nor cold, soft nor rough; and he needed *not* to know, so the winter couldn't freeze him nor the brambles discourage him. Touch. When was he ever touched? Tickled? Massaged? Caressed? We'll give him massages and baths . . . hot baths and clean rough towels! Feather beds and ironed sheets. Wake his nerves, his sleeping skin. His reactions should be interesting!

b. Hearing.

His hearing is acute in regard to his needs, but words, speech, language—these don't exist for him. My God, isn't this true of all of us? Would I sit still for a lecture in Chinese? What does Racine mean to an illiterate peasant? We hear what we know, because that's all we'll listen to.

c. Vision.

Vision the same. Attention! How can I get his attention? Stimulate his hearing and vision, somehow massage them like his skin. New sights and sounds. His needs! Connect everything to his needs!

d. Taste

Taste also. What child does not love candy? This one. And until he does, is he truly a child?

3. Give him new thoughts and ideas.

This will come, I believe, if the senses awake. His world is impoverished; how could his mind be otherwise? As he feels and sees and tastes more, so he'll need and want more. Sensations, needs, desires, objects . . . *needs*! Increase his needs. Where else do *ideas* come from? They will come.

4. Speech.

I want him to speak to me. I want him to tell me what he knows, what he sees, who he is. It will come. Babies imitate what they hear. When he can listen, when he can hear speech, it will come.

5. Thinking.

What is it? Where does it start? Out of needs and desires frustrations arise. We are driven to invent solutions. We draw on memories. We combine them and recombine them, till they become . . . ideas! Ha! This is what he has *me* doing! Why? Why am I doing this? What makes it so fascinating, so important? The challenge? Is it simple ambition? The satisfaction of proving them wrong: Sicard—the great Sicard—and Pinel and all the others? My God! How presumptuous! But it's vile, the way he's been treated, plucked from the wild and then tossed away like trash. It's an irresistible opportunity! If I succeed—if I'm right—I'll have proven something absolutely essential about man's basic nature: that we *learn* to be what we are. I believe I can do it! It seems so *clear* to me! And there's something else, something about this boy . . .

Itard is startled by the bells. Five o'clock. My God! Has the day passed? He can barely see across the pond. The boy is a pale blur, still motionless in the wind and rain.

My dear Dr. Pinel, Abbé Sicard, esteemed members of the committee, and of the Society of Observers of Man, I would like to introduce you to my pupil and protégé . . .

Isn't it amazing? In all these months, he hasn't been given a name.

10

Blessed Sunday.

"Eat, Albert! Eat! It's good. One more bite. Open . . . open the mouth." The infant waved his arms, turned his head, and Julie found herself offering the milk-sopped bread to her nephew's ear. He slapped the puddled table and began to screech.

"He won't eat any more," she said to Rose. "I'm going now."

"What am I supposed to do with him?" snapped Rose. She bit through her thread and stabbed the pincushion with her needle. "I have all these seams to do and Evelyn won't be back for another hour!"

"Let him crawl around and chase the kittens," said Julie, wrapping on her shawl and taking her bag. "Let him cry. I'm late!"

Out the door and down the stairs, she turned to the right and suddenly, a hand over her eyes and nose, the smell of plaster and Nicholas. A hand—large, callused, teasing—snaked around below her belly.

"My little bunny-rabbit! Where are you running, little bunny-rabbit? Stay and we'll play." He breathed his words into her ear and poked his tongue in after them and she had to laugh, it tickled so.

"Stop," she squealed. "I have to go see Mama and Papa. Stop, Nicholas!" He gave her a little pinch right where he shouldn't. She shrieked and he released her. She turned to shout to him but, seeing his silly grin, just blushed, and then, almost running, she hurried away.

"Come back, little bunny!" he called after. "Hurry back!" Why must he *do* that? she hissed to herself with clenched teeth, quickly flicking away two escaped tears. *Why?*

Once free, breathing the cold, pungent Paris air and clutching her small cloth bag, she raced along the icy streets and gutters to the Rue St.-Jacques.

She sped through the Luxembourg Gardens, the black, wet, naked trees, and then along the bleak Institute walls. This always seemed the longest part of the journey, all the way around the corner to the main gate. Passing under its great arch, she ran across the echoing courtyard, and then up the five stony flights to stand breathless, knocking at her parents' apartment. A woman she'd never seen before opened the door.

"They're not here anymore," she said. "They've moved."

"Moved? When? Where?" Sudden panic, as if she were falling—empty space, no one to catch her.

"They moved last week, third floor, the apartment at the

rear." Moved? What's happened? Julie raced down the stairs and was about to knock when the door flew open and her mother stood there smiling, drying her hands on her apron.

"Julie! Just wait till you see, wait till you hear the news! This is the doctor's apartment! Dr. Itard! He's been made the resident doctor, and can you guess who his housekeeper is to be? Can you guess?"

"Mother!" cried Julie. "Is it you?"

Her mother clapped her hands and laughed. "Yes! No more sweating in that dungeon of a kitchen, no more one-room apartment—and more money! Look! This is the sitting room. Look at the chairs, the carpets, the curtains—and pictures! Aren't they splendid? And here, this is the kitchen. What a kitchen, eh? *My* kitchen! Come, look at this, this is where your father and I will sleep. Feel the bed! And the bureau, with a mirror that tilts! And look at the view. And here! Guess who will sleep in this room, right next to ours?"

"Mother . . . is it mine?"

"Of course! For you and Rose whenever you stay here. Look, a window and your own bed and closet—and look at the bedspread!"

"I can't live here with you and Papa?"

"Oh, no, no. You know the rules—boys only, no girls. But you can stay for two or three days. I'll need your help with getting things arranged." Two or three days might even be four. Three or four days might never end.

"And here"—her mother opened a door—"next to us is the boy's room."

"The boy?"

"The savage! That's why the doctor is here. He's going to teach the savage to speak, to read—everything! And I'm to help, too, as well as cook and clean for the doctor! I'm to care for the child, to feed him, and take him for walks, and, of course, when you're here, you'll help also. He's a handful, that savage. Ah, my dear! We are blessed! God has blessed us!"

Julie looked into the room that was the savage's. A whole room. On a shelf, the little ballerina stood poised on its music box.

"The doctor! Such a good, fine young man. And—my God—intelligent! He's with the boy now, in the gardens. That savage! He's changed so much already, you won't recognize him!"

Julie recognized him. The doctor brought him in and he trotted around the apartment sniffing at everything. Like a dog back from its walk.

"Remember Julie?" asked her mother as he tried to sniff at the girl's hands; she hid them behind her and turned away.

He was clean. He wore a shirt and trousers. But still he rocked from side to side whether he walked or stood or sat. And still his awful eyes snaked over and around her without ever seeing her, without recognizing her. Yes. Like a snake. Why doesn't he go away? When will life be as I want it? When will it be for me? Just for me?

· · ·

The water was boiling now, and the kitchen steamy. They all watched the savage. Julie's father was ill again today. He sat with a blanket around his shoulders, his cup in his gnarled and callused hands. His gaunt face looked gray. Julie and her mother stood on either side. They watched the boy. Holding a basketful of potatoes to his chest, he carefully took each one, and tenderly surrendered it to the bubbling pot. Then he added wood to the fire, carefully, precisely.

"He's going to take over your kitchen, Sophie," chuckled Julie's coughing father. Itard sat opposite, straddling a chair, resting his chin on clasped fingers. His eyes on the boy. Julie glanced at the doctor from time to time; what does he see? What is he looking at? Mama thinks God watches us like that. Who watches me like that? Nicholas. She shivered. But that's different.

"Oh my God!" cried her mother and father together. Julie gasped. The boy had reached deep into the boiling, rattling water. He paused to look at them and then pulled out a potato. It steamed in his hand and up into his face, and it had his full attention as he squatted down and bit it again and again.

"Oh my God!" said the doctor. Julie and her parents looked startled. The doctor was not the kind of man to cry out or show surprise. He looked at Julie—his intense gaze—and pointing at her, he silently mouthed the words he had just said: "Oh my God." Then he pointed to the boy and back to her, mouthing the words again. It was a moment before she understood what he wanted of her.

"Oh my God!" she said softly. The boy stopped eating and looked up at her.

"God," said the doctor. The boy went back to his potato. "Oh," said the doctor. The boy looked up at him. The doctor nodded, pointed at Julie's father, and mouthed the words, Oh, God.

"Oh God," said Julie's father. The boy turned to him.

"Oh my God," said her mother. The boy stared at her, and blinked before he returned to his half-eaten potato.

"Do you see?" asked the doctor, not taking his eyes off the boy. "As I speak now, he seems not to hear me, but the moment I say 'Oh'—look! Or when any of us says it, watch him. He hears it. Also, 'no'—do you see?" The boy, his open mouth full, stared at the doctor.

"Why those words?" asked Julie.

"It's the sound, 'oh,' " said the doctor. He was silent for a moment, then shook his head. "Why? I wish I knew."

"This is the first time I've seen him listen to anything he couldn't eat," said Julie's father, and even the doctor laughed. Then they each spoke to the boy.

"Oh, what a good boy!"

"Oh, how handsome he is!"

"Oh, how well he eats!"

"VictOR!" The boy, looking from one to the other, turned to the doctor. "Good evening, VictOR."

Itard pointed and nodded to Madame Guérin.

"VictOR," she repeated. The boy's eyes shifted to her. She laughed.

"How goes it, VictOR?" said Julie's father, saluting, and he smiled as the boy turned to him.

He had finished his potato. He stood and reached toward the bubbling pot for another.

"No! VictOR!" Julie, her mother, and her father all shouted at the same time, and the boy turned, his hand poised over the steaming pot. He stared at them inquisitively, looking from one to the other. He paused at Julie. He looked into her eyes.

He sees me.

The doctor went to the boy and put an arm around his shoulders.

"Monsieur Guérin, Madame Guérin, Mademoiselle Julie . . ." he said, "I'd like to introduce you to my pupil and protégé, Victor."

It seemed to Julie that she'd been dreaming of snow. A white world, the air full of spinning flakes. And she was dancing. She was a ballerina spinning like the snowflakes, and there was music. Or was it laughter? Someone was laughing. She opened her eyes. The squares of her window (*her* window!) showed pale gray sky and falling snow. It *was* snowing! And the laughter? The savage—Victor. He had a name now. She heard her mother in the kitchen. She slipped out of bed (her bed!). Her feet touched the cold floor. She pulled a blanket round her as she tiptoed to the window, and looked down into what, yesterday, had been the gray-brown garden. Now swirling snow had transformed it into a magical stage, and there was Victor. Oh my

God! Naked. She had studied Albert's tiny thing when she changed his diapers—sometimes he spouted into the air all over everything—but this was a boy her age! He ran in circles, then leapt spinning into the air, and fell rolling in the snow; with sweeping arms, he scraped snow to his chest and scooped it into his mouth and eyes. From three stories up, he looked very small against the white, and she could only catch glimpses of the tail-like thing between his legs.

"Victor! Come here, Victor!" It was the doctor. Julie pulled back against the wall. Her heart was pounding. The doctor was in shirtsleeves and held his jacket before him. Weaving in and out among the bare shrubs and hedges that were filling with snow, he chased the boy all around the garden, first in circles this way, then that, and all the while Victor laughed his pretty laugh and his thing bounced up and down. Then he threw himself into the snow. The doctor tossed the jacket over him, grabbed up the bundle of black cloth, white snow, and giggling boy, and trotted to the door beneath her window. She had one last glimpse of it, and then, except for the whirling flakes, the garden was still and empty.

She suddenly realized she was shivering and her feet felt like ice. She ran to her bed and crawled in, burrowing into the blankets like the boy had burrowed into the snow; and when she closed her eyes, she could still see him—his body, white arms and legs, his buttocks and . . . it. She tried to see it more clearly. Nicholas, too, has one. Rose told Julie that she had seen it. He had shown it to her; it was big and funny looking. She also told Julie what men did with them, how they can put a baby in you with them. After a few minutes, she felt warmer. She heard the doctor enter the kitchen.

"Today we begin the baths." He was speaking to her mother. "Make the water as hot as is bearable, and I want him in it as long as possible."

"Yes, Doctor."

"At least an hour, three if we can keep him happy. Then we'll give him a good massage. We'll rub him hard; I want him to feel it. Then you can take him out again, and after lunch, another bath. We will do this every day."

"Yes, Doctor."

"Every day."

He sits in the water and the light, and again and again, his eyes follow the steam to the ceiling, where the light bounces and jiggles. When he moves his hands the light bounces and jiggles, and he doesn't hear his own laughter, only the water when he moves his hands, or when it pours over him, drenching him in light; water and light are everywhere. Hands touch him again and again and hands are everywhere as he follows the steam to the jiggling light, again and again . . .

"It's a carriage, Victor." Julie held it up in front of him. "Do you see the horses? See the wheels go around. They spin. And the little doors, see how they open and close?"

It was a wonderful carriage. The gold paint shone, and

the horses' manes and tails were real horse hair. It was a carriage for great ladies. For a princess.

Victor turned his back. He picked up a walnut shell, sniffed it, and then sucked it, looking for the nut. In the middle of the room, straddling his chair, chin on fist, the doctor watched. His eyes, thought Julie, are like looking into the night—like the night watching.

"Give him the carriage," said the doctor. "Let him feel it. He's beginning to feel things now. Give him the mane, the tail . . ."

Julie circled Victor to face him, and pressed the carriage into his hands. He got up and trotted with it to the far corner of the room and put it behind a chair. Then he came back to squat beside Julie in front of the fire. He hummed and rocked.

What can I give him besides food, Itard pondered, to engage his attention? I need his attention. Only his needs elicit his attention; the toys have no meaning for him. Food does, but he eats it, it's gone. It leads nowhere. I need something else. Something to give him pleasure, like his baths, his runs in the garden. Something that will give me his attention, arrest it, focus it, so I can expand it, reach into him and begin to fill him—with ideas, with words . . .

"The music box, Julie," he said. "Wind it up and let him see the dancer again." She picked up the music box and wound it very slowly. Her heart ached for it. It was painted with a shepherd and shepherdess in a fairy-tale valley. The dancer's gown was real silk and lace; her tiny wig was all curls. She held the tinkling, twirling thing in front of Victor's eyes.

He pushed it away and made impatient squeaking sounds.

"Oh! Oh! No! Oh!"

Julie looked at the doctor. His eyes were wide and he half stood over his chair.

"Did he say *no?*" he asked.

"I'm . . . I'm not sure," she murmured. He motioned for her to pursue the boy, who had turned his back again. She held the toy up to him once more.

"Look, Victor. Look—see how lovely? Do you hear the music? See the dancer?"

He shrieked and knocked the box out of her hand. It bounced across the room and she shrieked and scrambled after it. The dancer lay here and the box there. She retrieved the pieces and blinked back hot tears. The key would not turn.

The doctor was on the floor in front of Victor, pulling the string of a jumping jack. It was dressed in red silk: an officer of the guard.

"Look, Victor! Look—it jumps! See it jump?" When we push him, when he's angry, things happen. He said "no"! I'm almost *sure* he said it! He has more aversions than desires—use them! Victor moved away and the doctor crawled after him. Julie held the music box and the dancer. If she behaved as Victor did, would the doctor crawl after her? Would he look at her? Would she then live with her mother and father and have treasures like these to play with or destroy?

The doctor cornered Victor in front of the fire.

"It's a soldier boy, Victor," he said. "You can be a soldier when you grow up. Would you like to be a soldier?" Victor looked at the jumping jack, and then at the doctor. There was no escape. He took the toy, turned to the fire, and very carefully placed it in the flames. Then, taking two pieces of wood from the basket, he placed them on top, and knelt down, holding his hands toward the warmth.

Itard laughed—a brief snort—and shook his head.

"Well, that's new. You're beginning to feel warmth. It feels good, does it? Good . . ." The doctor sighed as he rubbed the boy's back. "Victor, Victor . . . What can I show you, what can I do? How can I teach you what every child knows—how to play with toys?"

Julie watched them as she slipped the broken dancer into her apron pocket.

I I

Flapping.
    Flapping.
    Flapping crows.
  Flying, flapping all around him.
  He feels the wind of the wings. Slapping. The forest is made of ice. The earth, the trees, each branch and twig are made of ice. The slapping crows are boys, the boys are flapping crows. Pinching, slapping, poking with all their fingers. He runs and scrambles, he huddles and claws at the icy, glassy ground, to be into, to be under . . .
  He opens his eyes.
  Gray light. He's huddled on the bare bed. The open window is full of wind and flapping curtains. Flapping. The wind whips over him, like slapping. Like the fingers of boys. He shuts his eyes. He sees a bath steaming. He feels round his bed, searching. Where is his cloth full of feathers? It smells of him. His. It is Victor's. He looks around the room.

On the chair his shirt is flapping. Victor's shirt. He takes it. He must find the inside. He burrows into it. Victor's smell . . . but the world is gone! He can't find the world! He hears the door open. Madame Guérin. Her odor fills the room. Her laughter is everywhere.

"Oh poor dear! Poor pup! Where's your blanket? Let me help you!" He can smell each of her fingers, her velvet dress, her hair. He smells milk and bread. He smells the doctor's hair and shirt. The doctor's hands. He hears his jacket and voice.

"Wait! Madame Guérin, don't you see? He's put on his shirt! Himself! I hid his blanket—early this morning— and opened the window; he feels the cold! My God, do you see? He's *shivering*! It's chilly this morning, isn't it, Victor? That's right, that's where your head goes. You can do it . . . You see? He can do it!"

Suddenly there is light. The world. He sees the doctor. He sees Madame Guérin.

"What a dear, good boy! To dress himself!"

"Now the trousers, Victor! Put on the trousers."

Madame Guérin and the doctor surround him with their sounds and odors. Warm odors. Every movement has its own smell. His legs find the insides of the trousers. He smells milk and he smells bread. He smells wood burning and water boiling. Warm smells. He hears water filling the big tub.

The bread is warm and the milk is warm. He puts the bread into the milk and then into his mouth and his mouth is full of warmness. He licks his fingers, Victor's fingers, and then the bowl. The bowl is warm. He holds it to his cheeks and eyes. Warmth.

"Your bath is ready, Victor. Come have your bath."

I was right!

Itard slid his chair closer to the desk and opened his journal. Each evening he had the pleasure of recording the day's developments: developments that, each day in profusion, dramatically affirmed his evaluation and his approach. Sicard, though he said little, was clearly impressed—and now De Gerando was interested. What a pleasant fellow! Not only brilliant, but available and friendly. I was right!

He finds he can't help but repeat it to himself over and over all through the day. And they were wrong! He dipped his pen in ink.

12 Germinal, Year IX

(April 2, 1801)

Just today, purposely, I heated the bath to a lesser degree— not cold, but less than hot. Maybe because of the lack of steam, Victor put his fingers into the water, to test it, and then pulled them out and looked at them. He showed them to me, but I pretended not to understand, and pushed him toward the tub. He resisted, broke away, ran to Madame Guérin, and held the fingers up to her. When she also urged him toward the bath, he continued resisting till, abruptly, his temper flared; roughly taking hold of her hand, he plunged it into the water and then looked at her expectantly.

"Aha!" she said. "It needs heating."

Now, after less than five months of work on his sense of touch, he dresses himself every morning, whether we take his blanket or not, and, always now, he uses a spoon to take hot foods from the fire or out of a boiling pot. This morning, after his bath, he spent a long while caressing Madame Guérin's velvet dress. I will begin to make the baths shorter, and the massages also. The massages of the lower back and buttocks, however, must be discontinued altogether; they are beginning to excite him genitally. How did that fellow Bonnaterre put it in his report on the boy? "Because of his youth, he is still a stranger to that tumultuous passion which torments, yet perpetuates, all living things: he has not yet felt the sentiment of love . . ." With his increasing socialization, puberty, I'm afraid, will come soon enough. And when it does? What then?

There was a tapping at the door.

"Excuse me, Doctor . . ." Madame Guérin's face showed puzzlement as well as concern. "Victor is . . ."

"What's wrong? What is it?" Itard got up and and followed her.

"He's sneezing and his nose is running. But such sneezes!"

There on his bed sat Victor, both nostrils streaming snot. He sneezed, snapping his head forward, then whirled round in terror, as if looking for the source of this explosion. Another sneeze sent him scrambling under his blankets, where he huddled, trembling.

"Bless you, Victor!" Itard laughed and applauded. "Bless you!" Grinning, he turned to Madame Guérin. She was startled. She'd never seen him like this.

"He's never sneezed before, even when they stuffed his nose with snuff. Now he's normal! A normal boy with a normal cold. Tomorrow, Madame Guérin, you must teach him to blow his nose."

He patted the blanketed bump that was Victor's head, and then hurried back to his journal.

12

People turned to stare at the young man in the top hat being towed down the street by a frenzied boy in blue velour. Some greeted them.

"Good evening, Doctor. Good evening, Victor."

"How's our young savage this evening?"

Each week now, on Wednesday at four o'clock, Itard, hat on head, appeared in Victor's room with the boy's jacket in his hand. At this sight, after the third time, Victor leapt into the air squealing and clapping his hands. Even while wrestling with his jacket, he was out the door, dragging Itard and weaving madly through the crowded afternoon sidewalks, heading for the house of Itard's new friend and ally, the Baron De Gerando, where dinner would include, in endless abundance, all of Victor's favorite foods.

A pleasure repeated, Itard had expounded to De Gerando, becomes a need, and each need connects us to the world in a new way. And so the baron had made Wednesday "dinner at the De Gerandos' " day—food as a social experience—and now, for Victor, it was a necessity.

Itard gripped the boy's wrist, yanked him away from food stalls, and did his best to keep him to a trot and avoid collisions. Everyone recognized the "savage." Some smiled, others stared.

"Does it bite, Citizen?"

"He's a handful, isn't he, Doctor?"

"Look! It's the savage!"

"How's your wild boy this evening, Doctor?"

Itard mumbled replies and nodded his good evenings. He was still uneasy with the Paris crowds; the unaccustomed attention was both exhilarating and unnerving; it made him anxious. Although Bonaparte promised a new era of order and stability, these were *still* the people of Paris, people who, just six or seven years ago, in the name of Freedom, Equality, and Reason, had slaughtered a king and queen, as well as thousands of their own neighbors. This, and the horrors he had seen in Toulon, always came to mind on evenings such as this, when the streets were crowded.

There had been gazette articles on his undertaking— "Doctor Attempts Education of the Savage!"—which, of course, were completely inaccurate and misleading. We are simply another exotic distraction, Victor, in a Paris that offers them in abundance: countless cafés, music halls, melodramas, concerts, amusement parks illuminated through the night; and everywhere, the women, women of every description, offering themselves at fees to fit every purse and predilection—a few sous to handfuls of gold;

none of which interested Itard in the slightest. Nothing could be more exciting than *this work*, and no one—not even Sicard—*really* understands what I'm doing except De Gerando. And the work is going well, by God—*amazingly* well!

Itard bounced off an attractive young woman in a blouse of transparent gauze, who cursed him under her breath as he stammered an apology. Victor had jerked him off balance and weaseled into a crowd gathered around a little table. In the middle of it, Itard saw a dried pea and three walnut shell halves. The world's oldest game. The pea was suddenly covered by one of the shells, flanked by the other two, and a chant in sidewalk Parisian French warned everyone to watch carefully. Expert fingers slid the shells around each other, slowly at first, and then in a complicated blur. No one watched more carefully than Victor, and no sooner did the shells stop and the chant become an invitation to bet, the boy reached out, uncovered the pea, and popped it into his pocket. The crowd burst into laughter, and the man behind the table suggested, through clenched teeth, that Itard take his chimpanzee back to the zoo.

"Come, Victor, there'll be plenty of peas at the De Gerandos'." Hearing the name, the boy was off again, careening through the streets with the doctor in tow. Yes, De Gerando was a marvelous fellow, an extraordinary mind! From a soldier who had suffered severe wounds and survived several close encounters with death, he had been catapulted, on the basis of a philosophic essay, to secretary of the Bureau of Arts and Sciences! His four-volume work on the formation of ideas won all the prizes—and he's fascinated with what *I* am doing! Just talking with him helps order my thoughts . . . and, of course, his financial support seems to have inspired Sicard and the others with a new respect.

Smiling warmly, De Gerando himself opened the door. Victor handed over his coat as he slipped past, already on his way to the dining room.

"Yes, it's going well. *Very* well!" said Itard. "This week we've been working mostly on ways to focus his hearing and sight."

"Those senses are very different from touch, smell, and taste, aren't they?" said De Gerando. "They're more directly connected to the mind, to thought."

"Exactly!" said Itard. "To reach his mind, I need to get him to listen, to look; I need his attention. But his attention is so . . . so slippery!"

De Gerando chuckled and threw an arm over Itard's shoulder as they followed Victor.

In the dining room, a laughing, helpless Madame De Gerando was being pulled past the sideboard—full of jellied candies, chocolates, and pastries—directly to the table where Victor had her uncover the various dishes so he could sniff at their steaming contents. At each of his favorites, his excitement grew. Lentils cooked with sausage started him bouncing; the whipped potatoes were greeted with little yelps of ecstasy; and the green beans and fragrant rolls set him pushing everyone to the table to begin the feast.

"Victor seems to be suggesting"—Madame De Gerando smiled to the men—"that it is suppertime."

Ah, Annette! thought Itard. What a prize she is. Her warm, cheerful demeanor, her intelligence, her trim figure and bearing, her shining blond ringlets. The perfect match for De Gerando. It was cheering to know that such women existed. Victor was seated next to her and, though intensely impatient, showed her what he needed and waited for her to serve him. Using a spoon and, more often now, a fork, he ate every lentil and bean with meticulous care, and none escaped him. He ate expertly and continually with a seemingly endless hunger until there was nothing more to eat.

"I think you'll agree with me," said De Gerando, "the older we become, the more we become specialists in how we approach the world. As a child I had to see everything, touch everything, taste everything, in order to know everything. Now it's philosophy that's the lens through which I focus my curiosity. Victor, at this point, knows the world only by smell and taste, and what he can put in his mouth and devour of it."

"I'd wager," said Madame De Gerando, using her napkin to wipe the boy's dripping chin, "that he would make a superb chef. Won't you, Victor?"

"I'd put my money on that," chuckled her husband.

"Of course," said Itard, "but that's too easy. He cooks now. As I expand his outlook and involve his other senses—when he can speak—he will achieve . . . much more than that. Much more."

When all the food was gone and his plate taken, Victor lifted his glass in both hands and held it toward the crystal water carafe. He watched as the glass filled, and then carefully sniffed the water. The taste of wine still provoked horrendous grimaces of disgust, and on his last visit he had mistakenly swallowed a mouthful of clear, fiery eau-de-vie. His eyes had bulged, and then, clutching his throat, he began running up and down the stairs. When that didn't help, he rolled on the floor till the panic and burning subsided.

Now, as De Gerando filled small silver goblets with Chartreuse, Victor took his water to the window and looked out. The day was becoming evening. He held his glass between his hands, and for a long while he sipped slowly, gazing out over and past the city, watching a distant hill fade to violet, and then gray, and then black, like the sky. He drinks water, thought Itard, the way a devout person prays.

A longing echoed in Itard. He watched the boy and swallowed a sudden urge to weep. Why these tears? He glanced self-consciously at De Gerando, who was busily scratching something from the knee of his pants.

Itard took a sip of the green liqueur. He studied his goblet for a moment and a thought startled him.

"I think Victor might have learned a game this evening—his *first* game. Victor," he said as the boy finished his water, "do you remember the game we saw?" He placed three silver goblets on the tablecloth, and then held up a chestnut.

"This game, Victor, might be the world's first game." He looked up at the De Gerandos. "In my village on market days, an old Italian—or Gypsy maybe it was—used to appear and set up his little table. Everyone would crowd around to play. This game is older than Paris, Victor, maybe older than the pyramids; as long as there are people, there will be this game. We'll call it Find the Chestnut! Watch," he said, though there was no need. Victor's eyes moved with the nut.

Itard set it on the table and covered it with a goblet. Then he overturned the other goblets, and, mimicking the street man, he moved them around and around each other, slowly at first, then more quickly. When he stopped, Victor's eyes flicked from goblet to goblet. He uncovered the nut and ate it.

"Bravo, Victor." Both De Gerandos cheered and applauded. Itard held up another chestnut. This time, he moved the goblets with starts and stops, back and forth, slowly as well as quickly, and for a longer time. Victor reached immediately for a goblet. There was nothing. He was startled. He peered into it, sniffed it, and then looked under another one and squeaked with pleasure when he saw the chestnut. He ate it quickly, and then looked up at the doctor. They played again, and the De Gerandos took their turns manipulating the cups. Victor kept his hands and chin on the edge of the table; only his eyes moved, flicking back and forth, and he found the chestnut every time.

Itard's hands were trembling slightly as he slipped off his ring, the one his mother had given him, and put it on the table. Victor watched him cover it, and continued watching as the cups whirled and skated under the doctor's fingers. When they stopped, Victor reached out. He uncovered the ring, squealed and sniffed at it, and, after handing it back to Itard, he crouched for another round.

It was played with a penny, and the next with one of Madame De Gerando's earrings.

"It's remarkable," she said, "how well he does."

"He plays!" said Itard jumping up. "Don't you see? *He plays!*" His fist thumped the table and the cups bounced. "I've got his *attention*!"

13

He looks at Madame Guérin, then at the water. The water is in a clear glass pitcher on the wooden table. He can see it and he can smell it. With both his hands he pushes his cup, Victor's cup, across the table toward the water. He can't reach it. He looks at Madame Guérin, then at the pitcher, and again at Madame Guérin.

"*Eau,*" says the doctor. Victor looks at him, then looks at the pitcher. He rises on his toes, and stretches his arms toward it a little farther. He looks back at the doctor and turns his cup upside down. He shakes it.

"*Eau,*" says Madame Guérin. She picks up the pitcher. Victor sees the doctor's glass filling. He hears the giggling sound of water falling into water.

"*Eau,*" says the doctor. He raises his glass and drinks. Victor hears the water in his throat.

"*Eau,*" says the doctor again.

Victor's mouth is sticky. He bangs his cup on the table. He bangs it again and again.

"*Eau,*" says Julie, holding out her glass.

"*Eau,*" says Madame Guérin, and fills the glass with water.

"*Eau,*" says Julie, and drinks her water.

Victor's tongue is sticky and swollen; it fills his mouth; his throat burns. Heat rises into his eyes and ears and forehead. He bangs the table with his cup and looks at Madame Guérin. *His* Madame Guérin. He looks at the doctor and at Julie. They all drink water.

"*Eau,*" they say. "*Eau. Eau. Eau . . .*"

Sunlight flashes in the pitcher, in the water. He sees and hears streams rushing. He sees waterfalls and bangs his cup again and again and again on the table till the pitcher and the water bounce and tremble. His mouth and throat and eyes burn, and there's nothing but the burning and the banging.

"Please, Doctor . . ." says Madame Guérin. "Please."

The doctor looks at her, then at Victor. The doctor nods.

Even as Madame Guérin pours water into Victor's cup he brings it to his mouth. Water flows over his tongue and down his throat as he turns to the open window, where he can see, far off, under piles of milk-white clouds, to where there are trees with leaves beginning. Water streams down his throat and he melts into water.

14

23 Prairial, Year IX
(June 12, 1801)

The carriage slows and then stops. The tall, black bars of the gates are gold-pointed spears. They are twined with ironwork vines and gilded flowers.

"We should never have come," mutters Itard, but Victor doesn't hear. He's sniffing cautiously at a white-gloved hand that has come, palm up, through the window. Itard fumbles through his pockets for the perfumed invitation; the hand takes it. Victor's suit is green silk and new. Julie and her sisters sewed it. Itard's suit is black and, as he glances down and brushes the lapels and knees, looks worn and shabby. The hand returns the invitation. The gates swing open and the carriage continues.

The long driveway is canopied by the blossoming branches of chestnut trees that tower on either side. The air, like honey, is sweet, sticky, and abuzz with bees. Victor is scrambling from one side of the carriage to the other. He reaches his head and hands out the windows. He makes sounds that are urgent and plaintive.

"Sit down, Victor. Sit still." All Itard has to do is rap on the ceiling and say, Driver, take us back to Paris.

"Victor! *Sit still!*" he says. He says it too sharply, and the boy's excitement doubles. My God! Why did I ever agree to come? So Victor can be gawked at again? Do I want their applause? This is De Gerando's world. These are De Gerando's friends. "My dear Itard, they must see what you've accomplished! . . . My dear Itard, anyone doing anything of importance is invited to Juliet's—artists, poets, statesmen, astronomers!" My dear De Gerando, what have I to say to an astronomer? Or to this girl, this Juliet Récamier, whose husband is evidently never at home, but whose salon is always full of celebrities, curiosities, and the reporters who fill the gazettes with their gossip. "My dear Itard! Juliet is a delight! Just nineteen, mind you, with the face and demeanor of an angel, a gifted dancer and singer, and an intellect that will astound you!" Some call her a whore and say the brother of the head of state does with her what only her husband should. What does she have to do with *my* work?

Itard mops the back of his neck with his handkerchief. He neither dances nor sings. He smooths Victor's hair. "We are to be added to her collection," he says. The boy is trembling and his eyes dart here and there, reflecting the blossoms that sweep by.

"Don't worry, Victor, you will charm them. You are a good boy, a fine boy."

The carriage has stopped. Itard's collar is soaked with

perspiration. The door opens. Firmly gripping Victor's wrist, Itard steps down, and then allows Victor to jump to the elaborately bricked drive. The house, as he expected, is intimidating. As they ascend the white marble steps, Itard's legs feel odd and boneless. A doorman in blue satin livery takes the invitation and shouts:

"Doctor Yzard, and his protégé, Victor!"

"It's Itard!" the doctor whispers, as Victor tugs at his arm.

In a long hallway the boy pulls him, zigzagging from one tall, arched window to another; their steps are multiplied into an echoey clatter. Overhead, on an arched ceiling, golden moldings frame a parade of mythological scenes; naked half-humans tumble through woods and in and out of clouds. In crystal chandeliers, hundreds of candle flames are all but invisible in the late afternoon light that slants through the open windows, and at each window Victor tries to leap out into the gardens.

Itard can hear a woman singing, and a harpsichord—or is it a harp? They enter a room, a blur of silver, mahogany, and silk. There is applause and laughter and another doorman announcing a Doctor Lizard, and someone grasps his hand.

"My dear Itard, it's good to see you." De Gerando's face glows, and Itard tries to return the smile, as he grips the welcome hand.

"And my dear Victor," says De Gerando, patting the boy's head. "How handsome you look in your new suit. Good boy! Come! Meet our hostess." He leads them both toward a young woman in a long white muslin gown: the Grecian style. She stands beside a harp as tall as herself. The room melts into a golden haze.

"This is our charming and brilliant hostess," says De Gerando, "Madame Juliet Récamier."

Everything Itard has heard and read about her is a babble in his mind. She smiles and offers her hand. He takes it. She is so young! Under a tumble of chestnut hair her eyes are playful, intelligent, and frankly curious as they look directly into his.

He bows and finds his nose directly over her hand—what is this scent?—and sees a drop of his sweat splash there. He loses the direction of the floor as he tries to straighten up, and finds her bending to his side.

"What a great pleasure it is to meet you, Victor," she says to the boy, who only notices her when she speaks his name. "Citizen De Gerando has spoken so highly of you and your extraordinary tutor." She looks up at Itard. "The baron says you're working wonders."

"Thank you, Madame. We appreciate your kind invitation."

Itard's eyes become entangled with hers and his mouth goes dry. He should say something more, but nothing comes.

"Please call me Juliet," she says. "You must meet the other guests. Come, Victor." She takes the boy's hand and bursts into laughter when Victor avidly sniffs each of her fingers. He then sniffs his own with equal interest. He sneezes sharply, and shows no further awareness of her or any of the others who cluster around, looking at him.

"This is Citizen Lalande, who is chief astronomer at the Paris observatory; Citizen La Harpe, a fine critic, a great poet, and a brilliant playwright who is also my oldest and dearest friend . . ." The names and faces and offered hands become a jumble to Itard. The stout, heavily powdered older woman is a baroness—is it Vaudey? Vaudrey? And there are two English women, duchesses, a mother and daughter. The younger one, after Itard assures her that Victor doesn't bite, pinches the boy's cheek and says to him in English, "We've heard of you in England also. Do you know where England is?" She looks up at Itard. "Does he speak English?"

"I'm afraid not, Madame," says Itard. "We're beginning with French . . . Victor! *No!*" Victor has taken hold of the necklace of pearls that hangs from the woman's neck. Hearing his name, he releases it. Itard takes his hand and the women surround him with questions: "What was his diet in the wild? How did he kill his prey, Dr. Lizard; did he hit it with a stick? Why can't he speak? Will he ever be normal? Why does he rock like that and make those odd sounds?"

Victor's eyes wander over faces, jewels, walls, rugs, and then he glimpses—through tall double doors that are swinging open—a table gleaming with silver and china. He slips loose and, ducking and weaving between legs and bodies, he makes straight for it and hops onto the silk seat of one of the chairs.

"Well!" Madame Récamier laughs. "Victor has found his place next to me." She offers Itard her arm and leads him into the dining room. "And you, Dr. Yzard—I'll call you Jean-Marc—please sit here, on my left."

Servants in silk pull back chairs. Itard sits and looks directly into the face of Citizen La Harpe. The man smiles or grimaces. His upper front teeth are missing and the hair that bristles from his nostrils is profuse and black, while on his head it's white and wispy. His shirt collar is not clean, and a large roll of papers bulges out of the breast pocket of his stained orange jacket.

"It seems," he says, gesturing at Victor, who is avidly looking about, sniffing for what he knows is to come, "it seems your Victor is already so jaded a Parisian as to be indifferent to our beautiful and gifted hostess. But tell me, Doctor . . . uh . . . Doctor . . . ?"

"Itard," says Itard.

"Tell me, Doctor," La Harpe continues, "does the boy show any knowledge or awareness of God?"

"I'm afraid . . . not yet," says Itard.

"Excellent!" says someone from the left end of the table. It's the astronomer, Lalande. "His atheism is a credit to his intelligence; it puts him far ahead of our friend La Harpe there."

"We can only pray," says La Harpe carefully, looking at Itard, "for the miracle that might enlarge Lalande's tiny mind and wit."

"Itard *has* done wonders with the boy," says De Gerando, who sits beside La Harpe. "Did any of you see Victor when he first arrived in Paris? He was barely recognizable as human. Now, after little more than five months, he dresses himself, eats with a knife and fork, and, as you can see, sits at the table and waits to be served."

"What has been your approach, Doctor?" asks Lalande.

"I began with his senses," says Itard, encouraged by his friend's introduction. "The boy had no awareness of either heat or cold. I began to stimulate his senses, and as they awakened, he began to experience new needs and desires. I try to use these as spurs to awaken his mind."

"This sounds like Condillac," says Madame Récamier, close beside him.

"Exactly!" says Itard, startled that this beautiful young woman—younger than himself—knows of the philosopher on whose ideas he has based so much of his work. Is it apple blossom . . . her scent?

"Well at least," says La Harpe, "Condillac claimed to believe in God."

"I search the heavens nightly with all my telescopes," says Lalande, "and I have yet to see anyone or anything resembling such a creature."

"According to Condillac," says Itard, "it is perceptions that give rise to ideas, which then, by means of language, are linked to each other to form concepts such as God."

"God, sir, is not a concept," announces La Harpe. "He is a reality!"

"And so, Jean-Marc," interjects Madame Récamier, "are you having Victor study Condillac?"

"No, no." Itard blushes. "I'm teaching him to play.

Condillac also points out that a child learns from play, and I've had to *teach* Victor to play—no easy task, but we seem to be doing it! I'm not sure, at this point, if anything one does is innate; everything must be learned, and there seems to be a crucial age for a child to learn each thing—to play, to walk, to talk. And Victor, you see, isolated for years crucial to his social development, finds it difficult to understand even the concept of speech."

"Well, he's very sweet," says Madame Récamier, "and he certainly understands the concept of food."

Victor quivers as a parade of silver platters are placed on the sideboard and uncovered. His nose twitches and he takes his empty plate in both hands and shows it to Madame Récamier. He looks longingly from it to her.

"Dear Victor," she says, "I'm glad you've brought your appetite—and your good manners." She nods to servants who bring platters, and she fills the boy's plate. Itard sees roast veal and squab stuffed with something, and the lentils that Victor will devour first.

"At least he has learned to eat real food," says La Harpe, as Victor's fork flashes between plate and mouth, "unlike our atheist stargazer, who prefers to munch spiders." Itard stares at La Harpe, and then at Lalande, who has burst into laughter.

"Spiders? Victor never ate . . . I mean . . ."

"I was telling everyone earlier," explains Lalande, "of how I tried to cure my fiancée of her fear of spiders. I went into the garden and ate one. It wasn't bad."

"And have you moved on to slugs, sir?" inquires La Harpe.

"My cook does marvels with snails," says Lalande. "I have no doubt she could do the same for slugs, though of course she will never approach the cuisine that our lovely Juliet provides us."

"Hear, hear!" says the Baroness de Vaudey from Itard's left. "But tell me, Lalande, are there spiders on the moon?"

"An excellent question, Madame," responds Lalande, and fills his mouth with squab.

It's difficult for Itard to keep track of the conversation and of Victor, hidden as he is by their hostess. He waits till her attention is on the boy, helping him with his food and addressing some comment to him, before he leans forward to peer around her, and finds himself lost in a tiny landscape where a shepherd sits by a fountain and plays a flute for a shepherdess perched beside him. She is receiving whispered advice from a plump, pink, winged Eros that hovers by her shoulder on a little cloud, all of it painted on a tiny oval of ivory, framed with gold and pearls, rising and falling on the creamy white beginnings of Madame Récamier's small, round breasts.

"It's sweet, isn't it?" she says, turning to Itard. "Has Victor shown any interest, as yet, in the opposite sex?"

Once again, Itard finds himself held by eyes so large and playfully alive that the possibility of disappearing into them seems a real and terrible danger.

"He is approaching 'that age,' is he not?" she asks.

"He may well be eleven," says Itard, looking quickly down at his plate, ". . . or even twelve—we can't be sure—but . . . he is still an infant in that regard."

"But how fascinating it will be"—she smiles—"when those tender urges and sentiments do emerge, to see how he expresses them. How do you intend to prepare him?"

Itard's squab has become a blur in the perspiration that drips into his eyes and even onto his plate. Should he use his handkerchief to mop his brow, or his napkin? Madame Récamier's question is one that has been nagging him all these months. He has given it much thought, but he can't find a single word to say. He looks helplessly across at De Gerando.

"I don't think we can really have any idea," says his friend, "of how puberty will manifest itself. We're dealing with the primal—and we've never had this kind of extraordinary opportunity to observe it uncontaminated by any societal influence. That's the adventure! But I will wager that with Itard's help, it will take a normal course, and give rise to new, sympathetic emotions that will speed his socialization."

"Ah!" says La Harpe. "But will it take the form of lust, or will it mirror divine love? My new poem—which I'm going to read to you after supper—deals with this very theme."

"You should be more careful of the manuscript," says Lalande. "It's sticking out of your pocket; someone who doesn't know your work might steal it."

"I understand you also treat the deaf, Doctor?" Itard

turns to his left, and the Baroness de Vaudey blinks at him with moist, pinkish eyes.

"Yes, Madame. I'm in residence at the Institute for Deaf-Mutes."

"How interesting! My poor Emile—my Pekingese, you know—seems to have gone completely deaf."

Itard is aware of shouts from the garden. He peers once again around his hostess, who is laughing at something Lalande has said. Victor's chair is empty. He looks around the room, and peeks quickly under the table. No Victor.

"Please excuse me!" Itard hurries to the window. In the fading blue twilight two gardeners huddle together. One points across the flower beds and holds up a piece of clothing. Itard recognizes Victor's trousers. Then he sees a flash of white streak across the lawns.

"I'm . . . terribly sorry . . ." Itard backs toward the door, mopping his face with his napkin. "I must see to Victor. He seems to have run into the gardens. This is . . . not at all like him."

"It's I who should apologize," says his hostess, rising. Her eyes show real concern. "I should have been paying more attention. Maybe the gentlemen would accompany you—in fact, we should all go." She gestures to servants, who pick up candelabras and form an aisle of light. "He is, after all, a child," she says, "and dependent on all of us."

Itard, followed by De Gerando, hurries through the glass doors into the garden at the head of a parade of guests flanked by white-wigged servants in aqua silk, each carrying a golden candelabra. He hears La Harpe and Lalande bickering behind him.

"The boy is yours, sir?" The question comes from one of the gardeners as Itard approaches. "I tried to grab him, and he jumped right out of these." He hands Itard Victor's torn trousers. Walnuts, almonds, lentils, and dates spill from the pockets.

"Please stay back!" De Gerando waves to the women. "He's lost his trousers!"

"Look!" cries the Baroness. "He's like a rabbit!" Itard sees a vaguely luminous shape heading toward the great black silhouettes of the chestnut trees that line the drive.

"Victor!" he calls. "Victor! Victor!" But the pale blur only seems to accelerate. The gardener runs ahead, and Itard calls to him also, fearful that, pursued by a stranger, Victor might never stop. But the gardener runs hard, and seems about to take hold of the boy's shirt, when Victor leaps up and, leaving the shirt behind, disappears into one of the chestnut trees: a vast, towering mass of darkness dotted with blossoms like tiny chandeliers.

Itard, followed by the others, runs down the drive under the thick black canopy of branches. He pursues a flickering shower of petals that falls as Victor crashes through the leaves, leaping from bough to bough and tree to tree until he reaches the end of the drive and the last tree. The guests form a circle around it, and the servants raise their candelabras in a ring of light.

But under the tree there is no light. Itard's blood pounds in his temples, throat, and chest. Each breath brings a sharp pain between his ribs and over his shoulders. He's drenched with sweat. He searches the blackness that hangs overhead, looking from blossom to blossom, like fading white fireworks, until he finds one, high above, that he knows is Victor. A pale smear rocking quickly back and forth.

"Victor!" Itard calls up into the tree. "It's time to go home, Victor!"

"Thank God for the twilight," declares La Harpe, "which covers his shame and protects the ladies' modesty. Oh, how I wish Rousseau were here! If only he could see this disgusting spectacle of man deprived of the benefits of society and religion. Here, Jean-Jacques! Here is your noble savage!"

Itard remembers the nuts in the torn pants he has clutched in his hand. If only I had a nutcracker; the sound might bring him down. "Victor! See? Here are walnuts. Look! Walnuts!"

"Please . . . can you bring me a nutcracker, or some fruit?" Itard asks the gardener. "Quickly! Please, it might help."

"We have cherries, Doctor." Madame Récamier's voice is close beside him. "Bring a basket of cherries," she says, and the gardener vanishes. Itard realizes that the scent he thought was chestnut is hers. Is it lilac? Gardenia?

"I'm so terribly sorry," she says softly. She is like a shadow that floats before him. The crickets and katydids grow suddenly loud. Then he can see her eyes. "I feel I am to blame and I will do everything possible to bring him down safely." She puts a hand on his arm. "Please don't worry," she whispers.

The gardener suddenly reappears, breathing heavily. Gripping the handle of a basket of cherries in his teeth, he scrambles up into the tree. De Gerando urges everyone to stay well back. He takes Madame Récamier's arm and leads her aside. Itard stands alone under the blackness.

"Come, Victor . . . Come! It's time to go home to Madame Guérin, to your bed! It's time to go home!"

The carriage doors slam shut. Itard's eyes close and he falls back on the cushions, drained of strength, of feeling, of sweat. Across from him, as the carriage starts off, De Gerando is laughing. He laughs on and on. The laughter subsides, and then starts up again, and on the floor, Victor, in his torn suit, squats rocking, embracing a basket; cherry juice drips from his face and down his shirt, and the pits fall from his mouth as he eats cherry after cherry.

15

Julie watched the doctor's inquisitive fingers probing slowly, expertly, along the jagged white scar that marked a line between Victor's head and neck. The boy giggled—tilted his chin higher and leaned forward. He loved being tickled. She shivered. Nicholas tickling.

Itard saw Victor's body as a catalogue of scars: bites, gouges, burns, slashes, punctures, and scratches, but this one was different, the result of intention if not resolve. The hand had been unsteady and the blade dull. Itard had performed some surgery; it was a profound and thrilling experience, cutting into living flesh—the blade must be exquisitely sharp, the feel of life pulsing just beneath it—but to heal. Not to kill.

"Savages!" hissed Madame Guérin. "Can you imagine? Doing such a thing to a baby? And leaving it for dead? What monster could do such a thing?"

"His parents," said Itard. "A mother, a father . . ."

"A mother, never!" snapped Madame Guérin. She tousled the boy's hair and Itard recalled an old engraving: Abraham and . . . Isaac, was it? The bearded patriarch, knife in one hand, the other over the eyes of the bound boy; the sacrifice, the lamb that God demanded. Was it the voice of God, or an old man's deranged mind? And the voice that stopped him—was that God, or reason? Or a lack of courage? Can the voices of God and reason be different voices?

"As far as I can tell," said Itard, "his vocal cords are intact. Let me see inside, Victor . . ." He squeezed the boy's mouth open and peered once again at his tongue. "Good boy. I can find no physical hindrance to his speaking."

"But, Doctor, he's a baby." Madame Guérin shrugged. "How long did it take Julie to say her first words? *Ma-ma.* 'Mama' was her first—was it a year? No, it was more! You were a little slow, my dear—almost sixteen months! Sixteen months of cooing, gurgling, screaming, crying. Oh, how you cried! Well, I didn't have much time for you in those days."

Julie watched from a doorway, trying to remember a dream. Was it last night . . . or was it the night before?

It's true, thought Itard. He's lived in society only fourteen or fifteen months—six of them abandoned among the speechless! The deaf and dumb! An infant, like a sponge, soaks up everything: sensations, sights, sounds, being sung to, talked to, crooned to—a little machine avid to know, to learn. But Victor, with his mysterious, unspeakable origins, was shaped by the woods. We found him fully formed. Speech is something foreign and new. And still! . . .

". . . and still, Victor," he said aloud, "you're doing well! You hear sounds and words, don't you? You hear, 'Oh God!' You hear your name! 'Victor' . . ."

Victor looked up and Madame Guérin chuckled. "Oh God!" she said and mussed his hair. "Oh Victor!"

Julie's dream was coming back to her. It was here, last night . . . something about an animal, furry and small. Very gentle it seemed; then she saw its sharp little teeth . . . But she'd been awakened. A sound in the night. Victor.

"He woke me last night," she said. "Or something did. And then . . . I heard him making this . . . sound." Itard looked at her and she looked down.

"What did you hear?" he asked.

"I thought at first someone was calling me, but it was him."

"What was the sound?"

"*Lli-li, li-li, lli-lli* . . . Something like that, over and over in his . . . squeaky voice."

Itard stared at her. "Your name," he said. "Victor was trying to say your name."

Julie shuddered. He was right.

Itard turned to Victor. "Julie," he said as he waved her closer. She approached slowly. "You like Julie, don't you, Victor? Julie is nice, isn't she?" Itard took hold of her arm and pulled her in front of the boy. Victor's eyes flicked from the doctor to her and back again.

"Julie is your friend," said Madame Guérin from behind her daughter. "Can you say 'Julie'?" Victor looked up at

Julie. He looked directly into her eyes and then tilted back his head and offered his throat to her. He wanted more tickling. She didn't move.

"Julie . . . Julie . . ." repeated the doctor. *"Li, li, li . . ."* Victor took Itard's hand and used the fingers to tickle himself under the chin. *"Li-li . . . li-li,"* the doctor went on, and then, suddenly leaning forward, he said, *"Lait!* He loves milk. *Lait,* Victor. Would you like some *lait?"* He released Julie and reached for the porcelain pitcher on the table.

"Julie, would you like some *lait?"* He filled a cup and held it out to her. Victor's eyes were on the cup. Then the pitcher.

"Madame Guérin, *lait?"*

"Lait!" she said, and took a cup out for him to fill. Victor ran to the shelf and took his cup. He held it out to Itard.

"Lait, Victor? *Lait?"* Victor clinked his cup against the pitcher and jerked his chin at it.

Did I really hear him? wondered Julie.

"Lait," said the doctor, *"lait, lait, lait!"* Victor said nothing. He banged his cup harder and harder.

. . . or was it part of my dream?

"Victor, Victor . . ." Itard sighed, and then filled the boy's cup.

Each night, in his bed—Victor's bed, covered with Victor's blanket that smells of Victor—the night doctor comes. The night doctor smells of warm sweat and fire and dusty medicine. He sits on Victor's bed and says Victor, Victor,

Victor, very softly, and Victor touches the scratchy black trousers. Like charcoal. Like night. He takes the night doctor's huge hand and puts his own face into it and breathes the warm blackness—metal and walnuts, chalk and ink—the world of that hand. He goes into it, into the trees, deep among the mossy roots that curve around him so he can curl small where it's quiet and warm and he can become darkness. The night doctor.

4 Messidor, Year IX
(June 23, 1801)

Today, after repeating *"lait, lait, lait"* at every opportunity for the past four days, and filling his cup again and again (I became concerned that the boy would lose interest in the beverage), today Victor held his brimming cup, drank, and from his white-mustached mouth came the word *"lait!,"* a sweet, wind-bell sound, and then again, *"Lait. Lait, lait, lait."* He spoke, and—I am at a loss for words! I can express neither my intense excitement nor my profound happiness and satisfaction. I called immediately for Madame Guérin and Julie to share this triumph; they ran in and were greeted by Victor with his entire vocabulary: *"Lait! Lait! Lait!"*

Madame Guérin, this good, wise woman who has been invaluable in reaching this moment, clasped her hands and burst into joyful tears. Julie, as usual, stared from behind her mother. Victor—our *dearest* Victor—drained his cup. He *speaks*!

• • •

Julie stares into darkness. It is quiet. Tomorrow she will again sleep at her sister's house, sharing a bed with Rose. But now she is here, and she resists sleep, so as to be here longer. She stares into darkness till she begins to see vague lights flashing and flickering. She is full of longings. If only! If only she could stay here in her own bed, close to her mother and father. Then she sees herself running free across a green meadow. Ahead of her, at the road, she sees a fine carriage. Her mother is leaning from the carriage window, waving and smiling at her. Nicholas is the driver in fine livery. He tips his hat to her. She is in the carriage now, next to her mother. She hears the clopping of the horses' hooves. She is dressed entirely in silk. Richly patterned kaleidoscopic peacock tails open into fantastic images . . .

"Lli-li, lli-li . . ."

Two notes, very softly, as if scraped on a broken fiddle. She shivers.

"Lli-li . . ." Her name, as a cat or dog might speak it if one could talk. Several times, on other nights, she had wakened to moaning sounds. Victor. Once, she had gone to the door that connected her room to his. Silently turning the handle, she had pushed it open a crack for her eye. The room, patterned by white moonlight and black shadows, had looked strange. Victor had been squatting on the floor, naked, rocking and swaying in front of the window, moaning up at a bulging moon. She had watched him for a while, hoping he wouldn't see her and not sure what she would do if he did.

"Lli-li . . ."

If only he would go away. Her mother, these days, talked more about Christ and the Virgin. They'd begun going to church—like before the Revolution, Mama says, thanks to Bonaparte. Holy Mother, please make him go away. You go sleep at Evelyn's house, Victor—you share the bed with Rose. I will stay here and sleep every night in my own bed. In my own room. But it's because of Victor—Victor and the Doctor—that they have this apartment, this room. Now he follows me and says my name. He wants to touch me. Yesterday he touched my hair. He tried to touch my knees. Like Nicholas . . .

Mother says I must pray for him, but he's not even a Christian. How could he be? He doesn't know what Christ is, or the Virgin. He's a pagan! Like a . . . a troll. He howls at the moon like an animal . . . He tries to touch me. If I let him, what would he do?

"Lli-li . . ."

She shivers again and then, trying not to breathe, she slips out of bed to the door and presses her ear to it.

"Lli-li."

She pushes the door till it opens slightly and hears him sit up in a rustle of bedclothes. The room is black and he is a black shape in it, but she imagines she can see his eyes.

"Lli-li."

"Be quiet!" she hisses between her teeth. "Go to sleep, Victor! Go away!" Something warm splashes onto her foot! She jumps back with a sharp intake of breath and shuts the door. There's an odd yet familiar odor. She takes another step back, and under her nightgown a warm stickiness runs down her inner thigh.

"Mama . . ." she says in a hoarse whisper. "Mama . . ."

Dark drops spatter the floor between her feet.

"MAMA! MAMA!"

16

"But he speaks!" said De Gerando.

"No!" said Itard. "No." Victor looked up at him from over his cup. "I was fooled, too, at first, and I was overjoyed—ecstatic! And then I realized: it's not speech."

"I don't understand you. He drinks milk—he says 'milk.' This is speech!"

Victor's cup was empty. He held it out to Itard.

"Watch," said Itard. Victor turned his cup upside down and shook it. On the table, the milk pitcher was just out of his reach. His fingertips wriggled for it.

"Would you like some *lait*, Victor?" De Gerando asked. "*Lait?*"

Victor ground his teeth. He banged the cup on the table and made small hissing noises.

"*Lait!*" repeated De Gerando. "*Lait!*" Itard watched from across the table. Victor ran to him, took his arm, and pulled it toward the pitcher. He hissed again, sharply now, through clenched teeth. He connected Itard's hand to the pitcher by pushing his elbow, and he pushed his cup—always brought from home—as close as he could to the spout.

"*Lait*, Victor? Shall I give you some *lait?*"

Itard asked again and again. Victor lunged forward and bit the edge of the table, then struck it with his head. Itard quickly filled his cup with milk.

The storm clouds cleared from Victor's eyes as they disappeared behind the rim of his cup, and all that could be seen for several seconds was the cup's bottom.

"*Lait!*" said Victor when he reappeared. "*Lait! Lait! Lait!*"

"You see?" Itard leaned toward De Gerando. "He doesn't ask for the milk no matter how much he wants it. That would be *speaking*—communicating a need with speech. He says '*lait*' as a kind of exclamation, a cry of joy. He says it when he gets water or his dinner or when we go for a walk. It's *meaningless* to him! He can hear and articulate more and more sounds, and that's progress; but it's not speech. Not yet. A bit discouraging, isn't it?"

De Gerando nodded thoughtfully. He filled the tiny glasses with eau-de-vie. "But of course," he said, "he doesn't have to speak. He has another language, one that no one had to teach him: the same one the deaf use, no matter where they're from. The language of gesture and sign. I believe we can assume that it's the *original*, primal language—crude, but very useful in communicating basic needs. As long as he can express his wants with it, he has no need to speak. The deaf are the same. Speech is for expressing desires, thoughts, emotions—things of which, as yet, he has no inkling. Ah! Look what he's telling us now."

Victor held Itard's hat and walking stick. He placed the hat on the doctor's head and put the stick in his hand. Then, dashing behind the chair, he vigorously pushed Itard to a standing position. De Gerando sputtered with laughter as Itard was alternately pulled and shoved toward the door.

"When it's time for his walk," Itard said over his shoulder, "he brings Madame Guérin her shawl, bonnet, and a mirror. As an experiment, I tried to get him to bring me my comb. I mussed my hair and pointed to my head; immediately, he ran for the comb—no, Victor! Wait!" He turned to the boy, held his arms to his sides, and knelt before him.

"Wait. We'll go soon. Wait." He guided the boy to a chair and gave him some almonds. "We'll go soon . . . soon." He pressed the shoulders firmly down. Victor put the nuts in his jacket pocket and looked away. He rocked impatiently but remained seated.

"There's one thing that continues to amaze me," said Itard, accepting a glass of liqueur, "his love of order, his need for it. And I think I have a way to use it. You've never seen him tidy his room—or the kitchen. Everything must be in its place, and it seems he's always been like this. Bonnaterre wrote at length of his meticulous procedure for shelling and cooking beans. It's still difficult to believe that this seemingly sophisticated behavior is innate, while other things—things we think of as *essentially* human, like pity, or affection—must evidently be learned."

De Gerando laughed and shook his head. "My friend, I believe that this work you're doing with Victor will completely revolutionize our understanding of the essential nature of humankind. Many will find it shocking!" De Gerando raised his glass. "To your continued success!"

Itard's drink splashed over his mouth and ran down his chin. Victor was tugging at his sleeve.

17

He's awake.

Victor's smell and Victor's blanket. He burrows into them. A fly buzzes through the light, causing the tiny floating specks to spin, eddy, and disappear. On the wall, pieces of light, like leaves—like water—move back and forth. From the window he smells sun, dew on leaves, horse droppings. Burning charcoal.

But the room . . . it's all wrong! Where is the book? The brush is where the book should be. The book is under the cup. Where is the towel? It's all wrong!

Victor jumps up. He moves quickly, crisscrossing the room—rescuing scattered things, returning them to their true homes. First the book, then the brush. Then the cup. He stops. His eyes scan the walls, the shelves. They meet no resistance. This is home. This is the world. No! The towel lies crumpled on the chair! Victor snatches it up. He folds it and hangs it on the rack. The room hums softly. Perfectly.

"Victor? Victor, are you awake?"

He leaps to the door and throws it open and he's swallowed up in fragrant, yeasty warmth. Madame Guérin! He wants to run and fly, yet be always in her warmth.

"Oh my God, what a boy!" She laughs. "Oh God, what a Victor."

"Oh!" says Victor. "Oh!" Her hair—usually twisted into a loaf and pinned to her head—is now long as a waterfall, and Victor wraps himself in it, breathing it into his mouth, sliding it over his eyes.

She untangles herself and goes to the washstand. He runs after her and holds cupped hands over the basin; she pours them full of flashing water. Cool water, cool to his face and cool to his eyes. Cool on his tongue and cool in his throat. The towel is warm and full of sun. Big breaths of sun.

"Now dress quickly, Victor. Quickly—it's late!"

Footless, her nightgown sweeps her from his room. He inhales her warm, bready wake and runs to his trousers. Each leg in turn is welcomed into the blue velour—like Julie's dress. JulieJulie. The sound has her scent. Is Julie here?

Victor looks around the door. Julie's room. Julie is not here. Julie's bed smells of Julie: pale soap, pale fine hair. He runs his fingers over the spread: furry places and nubbly places, like touching grass and trees he sees from the window. There are Julie days among the days—days that have her scent. On those days she pours steaming milk into his white bowl—white for milk—with the blue stripe that goes round and round. Sometimes the milk has a skin—like Julie's skin.

Madame Guérin's room. This is Madame Guérin's bed and Monsieur Guérin's bed. He throws himself facedown onto the spread and floats in their entangled odors, bread and sweat and earth and smoke . . .

"Are you dressed, Victor? I need your help in the kitchen."

Madame Guérin's voice. Madame Guérin's room! He mustn't be! . . . He runs to Victor's room. Is he dressed? The shirt! Arms disappear. Hands reappear. Fingers button all the buttons. Open the door; the kitchen fire glows. Madame Guérin glows.

"The fire, Victor. It needs charcoal."

Charcoal like the doctor's trousers. He runs to feed the fire. The fire is hungry. Victor is hungry. The bowls are heavy, smooth, and shiny; he puts them on the table. Carefully. Each in its place; and the knives and spoons, each in its own place.

"Good morning, Victor," says Monsieur Guérin. He brings in garden smells: earth and sweat that prickle Victor's nose. Fierce smells. Monsieur Guérin's face is scraped red. He sits and Madame Guérin pours the hot, night-colored soup into his bowl. And then milk; the milk curls and twists through the night, and it all becomes something else and steams into his face.

"Coffee, Victor?" says Monsieur Guérin. Victor covers his bowl with his hands. Once he tried it; it bit his tongue.

He sits and looks into his bowl. He sees . . . Victor! Victor disappears in steaming milk. Madame Guérin's milk. He takes the bread, and tears pieces—like pieces of Madame Guérin—and dips them into fragrant milk, then into his mouth. In his mouth they are like Madame Guérin's dark velvet dress. Sometimes, he rests his head in her lap, her apron dusted with flour. There are damp places from her hands. Hands that tear feathers from chickens and turn them to snow. Hands that reach in and pull out of chickens all the things that chickens contain. Soft, pungent, vivid things. Victor, too, can pull feathers from chickens. He does it for Madame Guérin sometimes. His fingers pinch and snatch at feather after feather, till there is only white skin . . .

"Good morning, Mama. Good morning, Papa."

Julie! She's here! Julie's dress! Julie! Julie! Julie!

"Sit down, Victor!" says Madame Guérin. "You are still eating. Just say good morning."

"*Lli-li.*" Soap scent, scent of pale hair—scant fur on arms and shins . . .

"Say good morning to Victor, dear."

Julie looks away.

"Julie!" says Monsieur Guérin.

"Good morning, Victor," she says. She looks into her bowl.

White skin. Milk skin. Monsieur Guérin's chair scrapes; he's getting to his feet. He wipes the coffee from his mouth.

"Good morning, Doctor."

"Good morning, Doctor," says Madame Guérin.

"Good morning, Doctor," says Julie.

"Good morning, good morning—good morning, Victor. Please, don't get up. Finish your breakfasts—I've eaten."

The doctor's hands are on Victor's shoulders. Heavy, the bitter smells. Metal, walnut shells. There are short, thick, black hairs. A tuft of black hair on each finger. A ring of metal.

"Are you ready to go work, Victor? Shall we begin?"

The doctor's room smells of coolness. A fly buzzes and beats at the window, at the sun.

"Victor," says the doctor, "I made this for you."

He gives Victor something.

Something.

It is a little wall—a wall he can hold in his hand. There are things on it.

> Scissors
> Ladle
> Key
> Brush
> Knife

"Here is the key," says the doctor. He takes the key from the little wall and gives it to Victor. "Now. Please replace it for me. See? It has its own little hook." Victor hangs the key on its hook.

"Very good, Victor! Excellent. Now. Here are the brush and the knife." Victor puts them back on their little hooks. The doctor takes the scissors and the ladle and gives them to Victor. Victor replaces them, each to its proper home. Everything has a home.

"Very good, Victor!" The doctor's fingers rub Victor's head. "Very good!"

Again, the doctor disrupts the little wall. He removes things. He puts them where they don't belong. Again and again. Victor puts them home. Everything has a home. Everything must be in its place. This is the world. Again the doctor shatters and scatters it. Again and again.

The doctor brings more things.

Cup
Bell
Pencil

Was it here? Was it there? Everything is lost. The world becomes pieces.

"Here, Victor," says the doctor, "replace these for me." The key, the knife, the scissors, the brush. Victor slips off his chair. He sees the fire. The fire is hungry.

"No, Victor! No!" The doctor's hands are on his shoulders. "Come . . ." The doctor's hands turn him around. "Let's look at the board again . . ."

Victor sees the hooks. Each hook is like the others. Above each is a mark. Each mark is like a thing. But not a thing.

This mark is like the scissors. Victor hangs the scissors there. The scissors rest.

"Very good, Victor!"

And this mark is like the key; and this one like the brush. Here is one like the ladle. Each thing is hung beneath the mark that resembles it, till everything is home. The little wall hums softly.

"Very, very good, Victor!"

The doctor is doing something. What is he doing? He takes the marks off the wall! The marks are like leaves! He jumbles them.

"Victor, will you please replace these for me?" He gives the leaves to Victor. Victor bites them and throws them on the floor. He strikes his fists with his forehead again and again. The world is broken! The doctor shatters it!

Everything is lost! Awfulness!

With his face deep in the bed, his eyes fill with cool, mossy blackness. He breathes the bed smell. Mushrooms, the doctor, buried roots. The doctor's bed. The world. Victor floats.

"Victor . . ." the doctor speaks softly. "Look here, Victor . . . Look at me." Victor turns and looks. The doctor picks up the leaves and brings them to Victor. "Please, Victor," he says. "Please replace these for me."

Victor looks at the leaves. One is like the scissors. He looks at the little wall and sees the scissors. He puts the scissors leaf above the scissors.

"Good, Victor!"

He puts the key leaf above the key. The ladle leaf goes above the ladle. Victor is good. Each leaf is with its proper thing. Everything is home. Victor is Good. Very, Very Good. He looks at the little wall. He feels, inside of himself, a humming. The doctor's arm comes around him. Warm sweat. Rough-smooth the doctor's coat. He rubs his cheek on the doctor's coat. He smells a peach.

"Very, very good, Victor! You have done very well." The doctor's words make the world hum. The words make Victor hum. "Because you have done so well, Victor, you may have this peach."

The peach. His mouth. Warm. Sweetness. Sun and the buzz of bees. He looks at the little wall and watches each leaf mirroring each thing. Everything is home and humming. Victor is good.

"What you have made," says the doctor, "is nothing less than a model of the universe. That you have made it, proves that that is what it is, and, dear Victor . . . I am very, *very* happy."

Victor is good. Victor hums.

9 *Messidor, Year IX*
(*June 28, 1801*)

I took a chance today. It proved premature. The continued success of our work with the board encouraged me to replace the cutout silhouettes on it with printed words. Confronted with this new challenge, Victor was helpless, and he responded with a severe tantrum that was much worse than his normal fit of fatigue and frustration. It reminded me of the near-epileptic seizures of his early days in Paris, when he was unexpectedly locked in his room or excessively excited by crowds.

I now realize that the leap from the depiction of an object with its silhouette, to its representation with a written word, is one that took millennia of human history, and takes years for a normal child, for whom language and symbols are, from birth, part of his everyday environment. Reading and writing are first based on the ability to discern subtle differences in abstract configurations—more subtle than Victor is now capable of perceiving. An alphabet is made of variations of contrasting shapes: A is a triangle—O a circle—H and E kinds of rectangles.

We need a new board. I envision a large wooden rectangle with—at first—three shapes pasted to it: a circle, a square, and a triangle, each equipped with a pin from which to hang identical shapes of cardboard. Color. I'll make them different colors; colorful things are more interesting to him—indeed, isn't there, perhaps, a language of color with its own vocabulary and grammar? I'll use the whole spectrum. Later, I can add ovals, diamonds, and different kinds of rectangles. These are not things he can use, like combs or keys. These are ideas. Will he see them? I will make the board this evening and we shall begin tomorrow.

It may sound an exaggeration, but I feel I am an explorer in some unknown wilderness: this boy. Each day, each moment, step by step, we move on, both of us, with no idea of what we might find or where we'll arrive by evening. But step by step, I come closer to the mystery— the Victor lost inside. To know him, to touch him, to have him speak to me. This is adventure.

18

The doctor's hands are white and smell bitter like almond shells. Like a metal ring. Under the skin, roots wriggle this way and that. It's the hairs that have the scent: the short, strong hairs on the backs of the fingers. There are woods and night in the doctor's eyes. So dark, so deep. Victor peers into them. Careful not to fall! . . . He can't see what lives there; what is it that looks back out at him? The doctor's face is smooth sometimes, sometimes rough: pepper sprinkled on bread. The doctor's shirt is white like sheets, like napkins. The doctor's trousers and jacket are rough-smooth like charcoal, and smell of dust, chalk, warm sweat, and medicine. The doctor's shoes are night-black, and Victor can see Victors in them: dark, black Victors with little faces and big eyes that look up at him. The doctor speaks and speaks and speaks. The doctor's voice pursues him. Sometimes Victor crawls under his covers, or under the bed with the balls of dust when he hears the doctor's voice. The doctor's voice brings things. Hard things that have little scent, that cannot be eaten, that must be found homes. The doctor's voice sends Victor here and there. Every day the world starts whole, everything in its place, and then the doctor comes. He brings strange things with no homes. The world becomes a jumble. Pieces. Awfulness. The doctor's hands enclose Victor's shoulders. They can push him down, or pick him up . . . The doctor's fingers move through Victor's hair and rub his head. He leans his head against the rough-smooth knee, he closes his eyes and sees leaves falling, all the different leaves—like the scissors, like the brush, like the knife, like the key—all falling into pieces.

19

Itard watched.

Hesitantly, tentatively, Victor placed the red triangle on a card of identical shape and color. Then he looked at the doctor. The doctor nodded.

"Excellent, Victor, excellent . . . Continue."

Victor studied the board; his eyes flicked here and there. Then he laid the orange triangle on its mate and, after a moment's hesitation, the yellow one also. Then he slipped off his chair and trotted toward the door.

"Victor . . ."

He paused but did not look back.

"We're not finished yet, Victor. Come back . . ."

Looking down, Victor began trotting in place. He slapped his thighs several times and then continued toward the door.

"We have more work to do, Victor—just another hour—then we'll eat. Come now . . ."

Victor's trotting in place became stamping. He shook his head from side to side and beat his thighs with his fists; then he threw himself onto the bed and clawed and bit it; he beat his head on it. Itard watched and waited at the table.

The tantrums were becoming increasingly frequent. This morning there had been several. Itard waited. When the fit subsided, he went to the boy and led him back to the table.

"Here, Victor . . . Look! Aren't they pretty? Let's see what you can do with these."

Itard had made the board on the table in the Institute workshop. His father, the master carpenter, would surely find fault with it, but he himself was pleased. It was divided into twenty-four compartments. Each contained a card with a different painted shape: circles, squares, ellipses, a variety of rectangles, as well as crescents, diamonds, stars, and parallelograms. Each shape was a different color, and the more complex shapes had more subtle colors. Some were the same hue, but of lighter or darker values; some were the same value but of different hues. There were dozens of cards. As a shape or a family of colors became familiar to Victor, it was replaced with others that weren't. Now, Itard gave Victor a blue crescent, a green crescent, and a blue-green crescent.

"Please put them away for me, Victor. Please put them where they belong."

Victor held the cutout shapes but would not look at them.

"Look at them, Victor. You must look at them to see where they go."

Victor looked at the board. He took one shape and held it to each compartment. His face became perfectly still. Only his eyes moved, flicking from the crescent to the board, searching, comparing. Itard saw him once again at the very limit of his world, peering over the edge. He found the green crescent's place. The blue and the blue-green were more difficult. He began to slap at the board with them.

"Slowly, Victor . . . You have time. Slowly! . . ."

Victor threw up his arms and the pieces flew to opposite corners of the ceiling. He flung himself on the floor, slapping at it and trying to bite it. Itard's jaw clenched. It was still early; they had been working for less than an hour. It had been like this yesterday and the day before. He watched; his fingers drummed the table. Victor flailed and howled.

Itard went to him. "Come, Victor! Enough of this. We're wasting time . . . Come!"

Victor kicked and pummeled the floor. It's getting worse. Worse and worse . . . Itard rested his head on his knees, sat beside the boy, and waited. Finally, he heard the clock ticking. Victor lay quiet, curled on his side, rocking. Itard looked at the clock. It had been almost half an hour.

"All right, Victor, let's go on now . . . We're almost finished. Come, pick up the pieces."

The boy resisted at first, but with Itard's gentle, persistent urging, he finally did as the doctor asked.

"This is purple, Victor—purple. It's pretty, isn't it? Like grapes. Please show me where it belongs."

Victor took the purple parallelogram but would not look at it; his glance darted around the room.

"Look, Victor, purple . . . You *know* purple. *Look* at it!"

With continued urging, Victor looked. He turned the shape over and over. He looked at the board and bared his teeth. He nodded his head up and down. His eyes twitched from compartment to compartment. He stopped at a purple square. He began to lay the shape there but stopped. He couldn't. His eyes flew off the board and he looked round and round the room.

"You can find it, Victor. You found it yesterday . . . remember? It's not a square. Remember?"

Victor would not look at Itard. He placed the purple parallelogram on the purple square.

"It's almost right, Victor . . . almost, but not quite. Look again."

With Victor's high-pitched scream the harlequined board flew into the air. Circles, triangles, squares, ovals, rectangles of every shade and hue rained down on the room, along with glowing coals and cinders as Victor attacked the fire with the poker, swinging it over his head, up and down, striking showers of sparks from the burning logs. He flung the poker at the bed, threw himself to the floor, and rolled on the rug scattered with smoking coals. Itard scraped and stamped at them, dancing around the writhing, howling boy. He saw white flecks of foam among the embers.

Victor's head—eyes bulging and rolling, foam flowing

and spraying from his mouth—whipped from side to side and banged the floor; his arms and legs, which had at first beat and kicked, now jerked wildly in all directions.

Itard swore under his breath, "OhmyGod! Again! OhmyGod!" Helplessly slapping his thighs, he stared down at what had every appearance of an epileptic fit.

"No!" he screamed. His face flushed red. "No! You won't win, you little bastard! I'll kill you first!" He grabbed the boy firmly by the hips, ran with him to the open window, and held him face first over the stone courtyard four floors below. Instantly, the flailing stopped and he heard—and felt—three sharp intakes of breath. The boy's body trembled and jerked between his hands. It seemed weightless, and Itard felt he could have easily thrown it over the horizon, or hurled it through the flagstones below. After a few seconds he yanked the boy in and slammed his feet to the floor.

"Now!" he growled between clenched teeth. "Pick up every piece!"

He released the boy and saw that they were both trembling violently. I am my father—he is myself! Victor's face was a pasty gray. His eyes stared blankly, the pupils quivered, and his parted lips were connected with white threads of saliva. He turned and, with quick, hesitant steps and shaking hands, made his way about the room collecting the shapes of cardboard—red, orange, green, turquoise, cobalt, ultramarine, Antwerp blue . . . Itard mopped his face with his handkerchief, watched Victor, and scuffed at black spots on the rug that still smoked and glowed. He heard the anxious tapping at the door. Then Madame Guérin's voice:

"Excuse me . . . Doctor? Is everything all right? I heard you shout . . ."

The blood drained from Itard's head and belly, leaving a residue of horror and nausea.

"Yes . . ." he said to the closed door. "Oh, yes, just another tantrum, but it's over now."

Victor, still trembling, had retrieved the board. He placed it on the table and now, with his mouth opening and closing and his eyes flitting back and forth, he began to replace the pieces. Itard watched him.

"It's all right, Victor," he said, moving to the boy. "You may rest now . . ."

Without looking at him, Victor scurried to the bed. He fell upon it and curled into a ball in the center; he burrowed his face as deeply as he could. Great spasms shook the bed and made it creak. Itard counted them—one . . . two . . . three . . . four—and then, one by one, sobs seemed to come up out of the mattress: five of them, until, with a quavering wail, a tidal wave burst from Victor's eyes. He wept.

The door opened and Madame Guérin was in the room, kneeling by the bed. She looked quickly at the doctor; he nodded and turned away as she gathered the boy into her arms and lap. She rocked him and crooned to him as he wailed and the tears poured from his eyes.

"Now, now, my baby . . . my sweet . . . it's all right, it's all right now . . ."

"My God!" said Itard softly. He swallowed his nausea. "Do you realize? He's weeping. No one has ever seen him weep. Children weep. It's good . . ."

He looked out the window, his eyes filled with tears, and the flagstones far below blurred. He clasped his hands in front of him. They were still trembling.

Move! Run! Trees and branches and leaves whip past. Between the trees he sees Julie running. He sees her and then he doesn't and then he does. Julie! Julie! . . . She doesn't look at him. She runs and Victor runs. Running and running. The woods, the trees, the leaves. The doctor's voice is here. *No Victor, no Victor, no Victor . . .* No matter how the wind fills his mouth and eyes, the doctor's voice is always here. Leaves and branches try to hold him, grabbing and slapping like the fingers of boys. He looks down. Oh my God! He's run too high . . . too high! Far below he sees Madame Guérin. Victor! Victor! . . . She calls to him. Leaves are falling and falling—sky leaves, cloud leaves, scissor leaves—Victor!—water leaves, night leaves, strawberry and cup leaves. All are falling, everything is falling. He wraps his body, his arms and legs, around the rough-smooth tree; the tree is melting. The more he clings, the more it melts away. Something big is coming, something fierce, and he is going to fall. There is an enormous scream inside him.

He falls . . .

20

She is bringing something to her mother. Something in a covered pot; she isn't sure what it is—something her mother needs. But she can't find her mother. She climbs the stairs, reaches a landing, and suddenly doesn't know where she is. She had thought this was the Institute, but it all looks strange. She'd better ask Evelyn, she thinks, and then a flutter of panic. No. Evelyn . . . might find out about Nicholas. Rose might know—but where is Rose? An enormous cat is sitting in the middle of the hall staring at her with huge, unblinking, yellow . . .

Julie opens her eyes. She hears Victor's hum, a rising-falling moan, like the beginning of a song that never continues. He's in her room again. The faint, violet light tells her that it's barely dawn. Aside from Victor, all is quiet. She raises her head above the quilt and sees him squatting on the floor beside her bed, rocking back and forth.

"What do you want? Do you even know what you want? Do you know anything?"

"*Lli-li, lli-li.*" He sing-songs her name in his surprisingly high-pitched voice. He is looking not at her but at the wall. He rocks.

"I used to be afraid of you, Victor—can you imagine? Now I just think you're disgusting and stupid. You are disgusting, aren't you, Victor? Idiot Victor. And my God, they give you everything. Poor, disgusting Victor."

Victor, without standing, shuffles closer and puts his hands on her quilt near her knees.

"*Lli-li, lli-li . . .*" He massages the quilt with both hands and watches his hands.

"What is it you want, repulsive Victor? You want to be friends? Do you want to play? What games do you know? Maybe you're just a kind of huge kitten. But you don't even catch mice or rats." She slips her hand from under the covers and touches his hair, soft and brown. She ruffles it and rubs his head. He raises his chin as if to display his scar.

"Tickling is what you want, isn't it? You like this, don't you? I know what you like to do to yourself . . . I know what you have in there, in your pants. Do you know what that is? You don't even know. Or what to do with it? What Nicholas wants to do with me if I'd let him? You don't know anything. I could show you. But I won't. I could tell you everything, but I don't like to say the words. And you're so stupid, Victor; you're so disgusting, and you have everything. They give you everything . . ." She takes a handful of Victor's hair and begins to pull and twist it. Victor makes a whimpering sound.

"Julie? What is it? Where's Victor?" Her mother is awake. Her father begins his coughing. "What's the matter?"

"It's Victor," she says. "He crawled in here and woke me. He tried to crawl into my bed. Get out of here, Victor! Get out!"

"My God, my God . . ." Her mother heaving out of bed, her father coughing. "He won't hurt you. Stop crying, Victor, what's the matter with you?" At his name Victor spins around and scurries to her mother's door and inside.

"Victor!" Julie hears. "You know you mustn't bother Julie. You know that, you rascal! Julie, it's time to get up. Go fetch the milk!"

Julie pulls her blanket over her head. She feels so far away. From everything. From everyone.

21

"This is the alphabet. It's yours.

"I've made it for you, Victor. These shapes are letters. Yes, smell them. They are made of metal. Each has a name and a sound. Does each have its own smell? And I made this board for you. This board with its twenty-six sections is where we shall keep them. Do you see, Victor? Each tray has a card with a picture of the letter: A–B–C–D. This was all made for you, Victor. They are yours."

The letter A—handsomely cut, cool and heavy—rested in Itard's palm, a silent sound. How beautiful they are, he thought, each with its unique profile. He gave Victor the A, and suddenly remembered that, as a child, he saw it as a house or a mountain; a snowcapped peak, or the peaked roof of his boyhood home. He watched Victor sniff the letter, look through the triangular hole, lay it on the table, and then pick it up again.

What does he see? What is it to see the letter A for the very first time? Does it mean anything to him? "Do you see a mountain, Victor? Do you remember mountains? A is like a little mountain . . . and B. What do you see when you hold this? Each letter contains a sound, Victor . . . a sound that speaks to the mind. Soon, you will hear them. Very soon. But first you must be introduced; you must meet them one by one. Victor, meet Citizen C. Citizen C, meet Victor . . . and Citizens D and E.

There were no more tantrums now; there was still resistance but it was subdued. Now Victor could weep and, with fatigue and frustration, he often did. But there were other problems.

Itard handed him each letter in order; each was introduced and Victor sniffed it and turned it around, and then placed it over its picture in the tray on the board. Each in its proper place.

"Citizen H, meet Victor. And Citizen I . . . that's my letter, Victor: I for Itard. And this is Mademoiselle J, for Julie. Julie . . . And here is your special letter, Victor. Here! This is Citizen V, for Victor! And there is its mate. Oh, very good! Now pick them up, and we will find their mates again."

Starting with A, Victor stacked the cutout letters in a neat pile; then he turned the pile over and began to replace them . . . A, B, C . . .

"Victor! You *are* clever, aren't you? If you maintain the order, you avoid the work—where did you learn that? That's *amazing!*" He tousled the boy's hair. "Who taught you that? Or do you simply know it?" Is it innate, the understanding of systems? This is truly amazing! It's the history of industry: perceiving a system, finding shortcuts! . . . "Who taught you that?" He gave Victor's head a final pat. "Well, that's not what we need today. Today we need to do the work."

Victor was allowed to replace all the letters before Itard removed them and shuffled them. When he gave them back, Victor tried to do as he had done before, but the signs in their compartments and cutout shapes no longer agreed. He was baffled. Avoiding Itard's eyes, he gently pushed the stack of letters away and turned from the board. His left hand slipped between his legs.

"No, no . . . you know you mustn't do that. You know that's bad. It's *bad*, Victor." Firmly, he removed the boy's hand. Some days now, he had to do this a dozen times.

"No, Victor . . . Look here! Look at the letters, they are shapes like the ones you know—circles, squares, triangles . . ."

Victor watched as Itard removed the letters one by one, and then jumbled them. He handed Victor the O.

"O," he said, "Oh Dieu! VictOR! . . . O!" Victor looked at Itard—at his mouth—and then at the cutout shape in his own hand. Frowning, his head bobbing back and forth, he scanned the board. He stopped at the C and once again examined the thing in his hand. His face became still and his eyes deepened as he studied the two shapes. Then, head bobbing, he looked further, exploring the trays one by one till he placed the O over its twin on the board.

"Good, Victor! Good boy! Now the I. This is I." Itard shuffled the cards in the trays, putting O between Q and C; E next to H—and again, Victor, his eyes flicking over the board, found the mate of each of the letters, and it wasn't till almost eleven o'clock that he began to fidget and whimper and, once again, the doctor had to remove his hand from between his legs.

"All right, Victor, enough . . . You've done very well. Very well, indeed! Come, let's have a run in the garden now. It's time to run!"

Milk light.

A diamond of light on the table. Victor puts his bowl in it. Morning milk light. He sees Victor in the bowl. Soon he will see milk. Madame Guérin moves about the kitchen, from here to there to here, stirring the warm, fragrant air. Stirring the milk. He hears the doctor's noisy black suit. The doctor is in the kitchen.

"Good morning, Doctor."

"Good morning, Madame Guérin. Good morning, Victor."

He has the letters. Letters in his hand! He puts them on the table. In the light. The milk light! Letters in the kitchen! Letters *before* milk! No! Push them away. Push them away with Victor's bowl. Hold up the bowl.

The doctor doesn't notice. He slides the letters around the table. There is the foot, L. There is the house, A. There is the stick, I. There is the hammer, T.

"Lait," says the doctor. Madame Guérin looks at the let-

ters. She says, *"Lait."* She gives the doctor a cup of milk. He drinks and Victor raises his empty bowl to Madame Guérin. The doctor jumbles the letters and pushes them toward Victor.

"Victor," he says, *"lait!"*

Victor looks at the letters. He finds the hammer and next to it he puts the stick. Then the house. Then the foot. "T–I–A–L." He is startled by shouts and laughter.

"Amazing!" says the doctor. "We struggle and struggle, and then suddenly—it's been just two weeks he's had the alphabet! Bravo, Victor! Bravo!" Madame Guérin and the doctor—their mixed odors swirling—surround him.

"Bravo! But look!" The doctor slides the stick to the other side of the hammer and then points to the house. Victor slides it to the other side of the stick, then slides the foot to the other side of the house.

"L–A–I–T."

Madame Guérin laughs and lifts him. He swims in her bread and milk; her bread-and-milk mouth touches his face, his ears, his hair.

"LAIT."

She fills his bowl with foamy, steamy milk—Madame Guérin milk—and he raises it to his face and it fills his mouth and over the edge of the bowl, on the table, he sees "LAIT."

"Good boy, Victor! Excellent boy!" The doctor's heavy hands massage his shoulders.

22

5 *Fructidor, Year IX*
(August 23, 1801)

"Naked, helpless, devoid of understanding, the human infant is pushed wailing into this world to somehow become the being we know as the crown of creation. We believe this is his natural destiny. But is it true, as many philosophers through the ages have insisted, that without the nurture and education provided by family, society, and civilization, he would belong instead among the lowest, weakest, and least gifted species on the planet? This essential question has not, until now, been satisfactorily answered . . ."

Too pretentious! And audacious! To assert in my first paragraph that I've "satisfactorily answered" this "essential question"—those old men will tear me to bits. He scratches out "until now," and writes "as yet" above it. The answer should be self-evident by the end of the report.

The report. Thanks to De Gerando's enthusiastic accounts of Itard's efforts, the Society of Observers of Man have requested that he deliver a full report on his work at their next meeting. What exactly is this young doctor doing with this hopeless idiot? Itard has spent his evenings for the past six weeks wrestling with this report; on Wednesday—just four more days—he must deliver it. Writing has always been difficult for him. Though it seems he knows what he wants to say, his thoughts, when confronted, are a jumble, and must first be painfully sorted into some kind of coherent order before he can even begin the agony of writing and rewriting, endlessly searching for words true to his intent. Making it more difficult are the new developments that continue to occur at an increasingly accelerated pace, and his excitement, which seems to overflow the pages and threatens the objectivity the report must demonstrate. In tone, accuracy, and organization, the report must be perfect.

"I have presumed to set myself two goals: first, to exert all my knowledge of philosophy and medicine to cultivate in this child the abilities, skills, and gifts needed to be a complete human being, and at the same time to assess his nature so as to learn exactly which qualities are innate in us at birth and which are acquired. Have I succeeded? The question comes too soon, and I would have waited and worked on in silence if I had not felt it my duty to my pupil to present the proof, proclaimed by what we have accomplished thus far, that this boy, whom I call Victor, far from being a hopeless mental defective, is actually . . ."

Itard hears the front door open and Madame Guérin's singsong falsetto: the voice she uses with Victor. They are back. Then, in the kitchen, the quick contralto with which she speaks to her daughter. Julie is here preparing supper.

". . . is actually an extremely engaging individual, and amply deserving of further education, observation, and care."

Yes! Now let's read it through again . . . Just four more days!

Unable to sleep, Itard has been in a turmoil of anxiety and exhilaration. Using his journals, which on rereading seem chaotic and confused, he decides and redecides on the report's organization, and then reverses himself. At first, it was to have been chronological; then he decided that, organized topically, with a section devoted to each aspect of the work, it would be clearer—except, of course, the chronology might be vague. Again and again he reexamines the stained, ragged pages of the penciled outline he devised at the beginning. Throughout these months he has held to it—a makeshift raft on a stormy sea—based as it is on Pinel and the theories of his guiding light, Condillac. Is it schoolboyish? Outbursts of rapidly scribbled prose alternate with careful, agonized rethinking and rewriting—is it sufficiently scientific, and at the same time humanistic? This sounds insulting to the committee—this is boastful—this is not clear—this is simplistic—this does not belong in this paragraph. Trying to write of his response to the tantrums and epilepsy, he winces . . . But he had been right; the boy was cured! Instinctively, he had done what was needed. Puberty—shall I go into it here? . . . No. There must be a separate section . . .

There is a tapping at his door and Madame Guérin looks in. Her face glows with obvious excitement and the heat. A fine mustache of perspiration beads her upper lip.

"Doctor! Excuse me, please—you won't believe what he did!"

"Yes, come and sit . . . Tell me."

"He's in the kitchen helping Julie . . . but listen! As we're going out for our walk, Victor gathers up the cutout letters lying on the table—the ones he uses to ask for milk. He doesn't even look at me—he slips them into his pocket with his wooden bowl and off we go. We get to Lemeri's house and he runs to Alicia—Lemeri's daughter, the one he's so fond of—he pulls her to the table in the garden and lays out the letters, L–A–I–T. And he sets his bowl in front of them, just like that! The girl's eyes popped, her mouth, too"—Madame Guérin mimes the girls surprise and laughs—"like a fresh-caught trout!"

"And then?" Itard has risen from his desk.

"Well, of course, she pours his milk and calls her father in from the observatory. And *his* eyes pop—just like his daughter's!" She roars with laughter. Itard is laughing, too.

"No, Victor!" Julie's voice from the kitchen. "No! Don't!"

Itard's laughter is replaced with a look of concern. Madame Guérin nods.

"He did it at Lemeri's, too . . ."

"What did he do?"

"Put his hands in his pants. I take his hand away; he puts it back." She shrugs.

"And the others? He . . . touches them?"

"Oh, yes. Alicia . . . and Lemeri himself."

"Where?"

"Knees, arms, shoulders—patting—like he does with us. No worse."

The doctor rubs his chin and notices his ink-stained fingers. He looks down at the scrawled papers that cover his desk like fallen leaves: words, lines—whole paragraphs—scratched out and rewritten in margins, between lines, and on scraps pinned to the original.

"No, Victor!" Julie's voice again. "Stop that!"

"I'd better go," says Madame Guérin.

The door closes behind her and Itard paces the room. He looks out the window. There are fine, tall clouds over the green woods south of the city. A flutter of panic takes his breath away, as if he'd glimpsed the rising of a vast black storm. Puberty. Nature reasserting herself. What to do . . . what to do? Everything else is going so well . . . It will take its course and it will pass . . .

Just yesterday morning, when Victor's hand slipped down, grasping himself between his legs, Itard thought: I am his teacher. I am a doctor and scientist—a philosopher. Let's see where this behavior leads; perhaps, if I can direct it, other impulses—finer, more tender feelings—will be freed . . .

But as he watched the boy's hand, kneading and rubbing, Itard's own discomfort increased, and when the soft, whimpering grunts began to accompany the movements, he suddenly remembered himself, back at school in Riez, in the privy, and, as in his mind they all watched him—his uncle, who was canon, with disbelief, his mother with pure horror, his father with disgust and amusement—he could not help but continue his own movements till the amazing, awful spasm burst, and he became a billion stars falling through infinite blackness. It was an experiment he repeated only once more, to the same unnerving effect. The nausea, vertigo, and terror that had followed both occasions came forcefully back as Victor's whimpers quickened.

"Enough! Enough . . . Come . . . We'll run in the garden! Come! We'll run together!"

Victor had burst into tears and his nose started bleeding, but they'd run in the garden. Certain behavior is not permitted. This has been true all along. He must use the chamber pot. He must wear clothes. No, Victor . . . you must not do that. That is disgusting behavior, Victor. But he does it. The urges are so strong, and he has no idea what they are for or what to do with them. And if I showed him? If he knew? What would keep him from . . . Itard shuddered. Toulon after the siege . . . From the window of the hospital he'd watched six soldiers do things to two screaming girls. Things he wished he'd never seen. In the street! In the afternoon!

He squeezed his eyes tight and shook his head. Nature! Rousseau deceived himself—and everyone else. Society provides our only defense. For me, puberty was like a volcano suddenly exploding—*terrifying* to be taken over by a force that is not oneself. But with work and prayer—my studies—thank God, it subsided. I avoided those boys who gave over to it. Brothels! Awful, terrifying . . . Toulon! Nature is blind and brutal. We clothe ourselves in fine sentiments and tender emotions . . . Victor! Victor! Victor! What shall we do with you? He touches Julie—but he touches me the same way! He likes women; they're kind to him, they show him attention, but the touching—man or woman—it doesn't seem to matter! Is that the truth of us . . . of me? Where is that "tender passion"? If it must be learned, was it ever taught to me? What to do?

It's a race; education matched against the most primal urges, forces to which we *all* are subject . . . all the brilliant and esteemed members of the Society. Oh, to show them the truth! This boy, citizens, this boy is what we are!

He laughs, and glances in the mirror on the way back to his desk. His hair is disheveled, his face contorted and smeared with ink. He laughs, as always, without smiling; a short laugh like a bark. "Jean-Marc," he hears his mother say, "you should smile more!" He laughs again. Then he picks up his pen.

"No, Victor! You may *not* touch me!"

When he'd come back from his walk he'd crouched, staring at the fire, saying *"lli-li"* over and over, grunting and moaning and pulling at himself as if searching for something, or trying to tear something away. It was disgusting. Then he had come over and begun to pat her knee. Nobody may touch me! No more!

"Help me with these string beans. Come on, Victor, take

some beans!" Victor's letters lay on the table. I–A–T–L. Julie reached out and moved them around till she knew they said LAIT.

"See, Victor? I can do it, too." And what other words could be made? A–I–L. Was that a word? L–A was a word! She knew she could learn to read and write very quickly if only someone showed her a little more. Nicholas! Again and again she'd asked him to teach her . . . "Oh, reading, reading—reading's no fun, little duck. I'll teach you something a lot more fun than reading, little bunny-rabbit . . . Come sit on my lap. Come on . . ." They were alone and he grabbed her—*really* grabbed her; he held both her hands in one of his and his other hand slipped between her legs and he wormed his fingers into her . . . It *hurt*! He wouldn't stop. She struggled and pleaded and wept and he mumbled things and licked her ears and neck and Albert started crying; and then Evelyn was there screaming and slapping at him and Julie ran into her room. It was a long time before she could get her breath.

She had made her own alphabet: large letters she'd copied and drawn with chalk on the pages of an old almanac, and then cut out with shears. Not so fine as Victor's metal ones, but she could carry them with her in her apron pockets. She had forgotten them today.

All the words in the world were somewhere in her alphabet.

"Victor, no! Come take some beans now!" Victor, Victor—dog-like Victor. He makes one word and everyone falls over dead! She could make her name, and her sisters' names. Look! One of the string beans is a J. A string-bean alphabet! These two make U, and these two L . . .

"*Lli-li. Lli-li . . .*" Victor was beside her, one hand still in his pants, the other holding up his bowl. He had seen his letters on the table. L-A-I-T. He shook the bowl in her face.

"Get away! I don't wait on you!" He blinked at each word. "I don't take care of *you*! You're dirty! Go away!" He moved backward, looking at her.

"What's he doing?" Her mother swept into the room. "What is it, Victor?"

"He tried to touch me again." She glanced down at the table, at her string-bean writing.

"He doesn't hurt you. I'm surprised he goes near you, the way you treat him. What is it, Victor—take your hand away from there, you devil. You want more milk? I see you wrote it again." She smiled and took the pitcher from the shelf.

"I wrote it," said Julie. "I can write it, too. And, Mama . . . look!"

Madame Guérin, pouring milk, glanced sideways at the table.

"Ah, your name. Nicholas taught you?"

"Nicholas . . . is a pig. I made my own alphabet out of cut paper. I'll bring it, maybe you can show me more . . ."

"Maybe, maybe," said her mother, "but right now, soup needs making. The doctor needs his dinner. You should see him! Ink on his nose, on his ears . . ." She laughed. "If I didn't pull him out of there he'd forget to eat. But Victor wouldn't, would you, Victor? Now stop that! Wash your hands like the doctor showed you and help Julie with the beans."

"I'm going to learn to read," said Julie. "I'll teach myself; it's not so difficult. Writing, too. Look, Mama, I can make all the letters with string beans . . ."

Her mother moved through the kitchen, and potatoes and onions seemed to appear and peel and slice themselves. "Reading is nice for the ladies and the merchants' wives, but it never did me any good—not that I read that well, but I read enough—the almanac, the gazette. You can hear the same things in the marketplace and they're more likely to be true. Fancy stitching, that's what you need to know—embroidery—so you can work for one of the fine couturiers, not housework like me . . . No, Victor! That's nasty!" She was around the table in two steps and pulled his hands from between his legs while she spoke directly into his face. "You're terrible today!" He turned his back and moved toward the corner, grunting and moaning.

"I see you there—here, take more beans." She filled her apron and intercepted him. He spun around and with a shriek knocked the beans into the air. For an instant they seemed to disappear. Then they were falling all over the kitchen.

Julie burst into laughter and Victor began stamping his feet and beating his temples with his fists.

"Enough, both of you!" snapped Madame Guérin. "It's like Bicêtre here!" She took hold of Victor's wrists. "Julie, pick up the beans. Victor, calm, calm. Stop now . . ."

Immobilized in Madame Guérin's grip, Victor's flailing slowly subsided, and small spasms began to convulse his chest and throat. They became sobs. Then he stood there, bawling like a baby calf.

23

9 *Fructidor Year IX*
(August 27, 1801)

"Esteemed members of the Society, colleagues and fellow citizens:

"Naked, helpless, devoid of understanding, the human infant is pushed wailing into this world to somehow become the being we know as the crown of creation. We believe this is his natural destiny. But is it true, as many philosophers through the ages have insisted, that without the nurture and education provided by family, society, and civilization, he would belong instead among the lowest, weakest, and least gifted species on the planet?"

Itard paused for a sip of water. A drop of sweat from his chin fell heavily onto the paper. Destiny began to dissolve. He glanced up at the hall. There, looking at him, sat Pinel, almost exactly where he himself had sat just months ago. A few brief months. There was absolute silence. My God! I have their attention!

"I intend to describe here the course of the changes that

have taken place in the mind of the Savage of Aveyron, rather than merely an account of my own efforts . . ."

As he read, the trembling in his fingers diminished. His text took him over: a small, pale young man with an imposing nose and dark, deep-set, unwavering eyes, his brows dripping with sweat.

"My first challenge was to transform the boy from a solitary being into a social one.

"Here was a child, a complete innocent in every regard, plucked from the isolation of his rough Eden, and thrust suddenly into a completely alien, and for him incomprehensible, world where he was deprived of liberty, subjected to the curiosity of adults and the cruelty of children. He was then burdened with the most unrealistic expectations, and when he failed to satisfy them, he was punished with neglect and indifference and seemed most likely to end his days in the dungeons of Bicêtre. This is the condition in which I found him. By what right did society brutalize him in this manner? . . .

"Since his experience of human society had been, for the most part, painful, my first intention was to make it as pleasurable as possible. A great deal of the success of this effort has been due to the tender care, wisdom, and endless patience provided by Madame Guérin, who was assigned by the administration to see to the boy's needs. She now provides, in abundance, all he wants of his favorite foods, along with all he might lack of maternal love and instruction. I allowed him, also, plenty of freedom and accompanied him on runs in the country, which, especially in strong wind or changing light, afforded him such delight, I came to enjoy them almost as much as he . . .

"My second task was to awaken his senses and nervous system.

"It had been apparent from the time the boy was captured that there was something very unusual in the functioning of his senses; he was obviously indifferent to both extremes of heat or cold, seemed to experience neither pleasure nor pain, and was thought, at first, to be deaf because of his lack of response to even the loudest sounds. He provided living proof for those physiologists who claim that the degree of a subject's physical sensitivity is always equal to the degree of his civilization.

"To awaken and sensitize his skin, I prescribed daily baths in very hot water for as much as two or three hours, as well as vigorous daily massages of his entire body, including the lumbar regions. These last, however, were discontinued when it was seen that they stimulated the organs of procreation, and might, therefore, tend to hasten the progress of puberty, signs of which are already abundant . . . I also found that of his emotions, which at this time seemed to be only two—joy or anger produced by frustration—the latter could be used to push him to new levels of sensitivity and understanding . . .

"I provoke this anger, and even rage, only rarely, because it is a powerful tool, and, of course, I always resolve it in a just manner. On the other hand, I do everything possible to give him pleasure. This is easy enough: light sparkling in a glass of water or its reflection dancing on the wall, his own reflection in a polished spoon—any of these are enough to cause him the most delirious rapture . . . After just three months, he is now aware of the most subtle differences of temperature and texture; he avoids drafts and chill and enjoys especially the feel of velvet . . .

"I next began increasing the number and nature of his needs in order to expand his mind.

"I have become convinced that the intellect expands with the number and complexity of the needs one is driven to satisfy. I had only to repeat, once or twice, something that gave Victor pleasure and it became a need. Dining out with friends became such a need . . . The visits he makes daily with Madame Guérin to the Luxembourg Gardens have become another need . . . Madame Guérin herself, with all the attention and tender care she lavishes on him, has become a need, as is obvious when one sees the joy with which he always greets her, and his anxious concern when they part . . . His need for me is quite different, of course, in that our work together brings a different kind of reward, one that is not always experienced immediately. There are times, however, when we meet as something other than teacher and pupil, as in the evenings when I visit him in his bed. He embraces me and takes one of my hands, which he clasps over his eyes and holds there, sometimes for as long as an hour. There are those who may object to these intimacies, saying they are inappropriate; I indulge them without restraint, believing that he was deprived of such as an infant and therefore deserves them now . . ."

Itard looked up and nodded solemnly as he mopped his

brow. Then he plunged on, reliving his exaltation at Victor's first manifestations of speech, his discovery of Victor's innate sense of order and the matching games he had devised to exploit it, first with shapes and colors, and then with letters of the alphabet. Itard was no longer reading—he was telling.

"But as the pace of progress accelerated, so did an opposing force of resistance which took a variety of forms, the most serious of which was the reappearance of fits resembling epilepsy, similar to those the boy suffered when he first arrived in Paris. These fits increased in frequency and violence until further work became impossible. I feared a final impasse, and that the boy would become a hopeless epileptic. Increased kindness and patience were seen in this case to be of no avail, and so, as a last resort, I came to a remedy involving fear . . ."

There was a fluttering in Itard's belly. He was about to lie—not as to what had happened but only as to how it had come about. It was essential, he had decided, not to call into question a tactic that had proved highly effective. *That* was the important thing! What difference did it really make that it was born of rage rather than reason? The fact that he'd lost his temper—as *anyone* would—should not become the issue. It worked, and might just as well have happened as he was about to describe it:

"One morning, when the boy threw himself down and began to flail and froth, I *pretended* rage with scowls and shouting and, seizing him firmly by the hips, I held him out the window, facedown over the cobbled courtyard four floors below. He quieted immediately and I brought him in. He was very pale, in a cold sweat and extremely shaken, and it was on this occasion that I saw him weep for the very first time . . ."

Itard felt slightly ill. With the telling came a realization: he was terrified of his own rage and horrified by what he had done. That was why he had lied. He shut his eyes, took a breath, and continued:

"We resumed our work, the epileptic tantrums disappeared, and progress continued. A degree of resistance still remains, whether to diminish and fade or to emerge in some new form, we shall see . . .

"Just last week, before Victor went off on his daily outing with Madame Guérin to visit our friend Citizen Lemeri and his daughters, he pocketed several cutout letters of the alphabet that we use in our work. No sooner had he arrived at Lemeri's house, where he is accustomed to receiving refreshment, than he placed the letters on the table so as to spell the word L–A–I–T.

"At this point, rather than go back and summarize, as I had originally intended, I'd like to stop with this last accomplishment. To me it states, more clearly than anything else I might say, what has been achieved, and it also stands as a promise of much more to come.

"It is now proven that my pupil, Victor, a child who each day cheerfully performs many useful tasks for himself and others, is also able to focus his attention, remember facts, apply himself, and is therefore deserving of further instruction and education. And this is the same child who just nine short months ago was called the Savage of Aveyron and judged incapable of improvement.

"On the basis of these accomplishments, I believe there are several conclusions that may now be drawn; they are basically the same ones Locke and Condillac arrived at solely by the exercise of their intellects.

"First, that so-called natural man, uneducated and unsocialized, contrary to what some have expounded, is actually inferior in every way to many animals. It is also clear that man's ceaseless urge to strive for progress in the physical and moral realms is not inherent but learned in the context of society and a civilization. Further, that what the human infant *does* have in abundance is the enormous capacity for learning and imitating, especially in the acquisition of speech, and if this capacity is not used, as in the case of isolation, the capacity diminishes with time and with age. It is also now obvious that man's ideas and mind expand in direct proportion to his needs; the greater and more complex the needs, the greater the civilization. And finally, that the teacher, to be successful, must learn from each individual student what educational approach is most appropriate to that student, and what degree and kind of progress should be expected.

"Regarding other aspects of my pupil's development, such as his puberty, which, for some weeks now, has been manifesting itself with disturbing force, more time is needed before I can tell you anything conclusive; what I have seen already, however, points in a direction that may expose as illusions many of society's most cherished beliefs regarding the tender emotions between men and women. Because of the far-reaching consequences of such conclusions, I will wait until the process has run its course, and, until then, I will say no more."

His voice was all but gone. He looked up at all the faces, all the open mouths and eyes, looking back at him.

"I thank you, Citizens, for your generous attention." His handkerchief needed wringing out. His shirt was soaked. "Are there any questions?"

There was the scrape of a chair as De Gerando stood and began to applaud, and then they were all applauding, and more chairs scraping and others standing. Shouts of "Well done!" and "Bravo!" were mixed with the applause and Itard felt himself blush as a wonderful sensation of vibrating warmth filled his groin, belly, and chest, and it seemed to him that there was a tremendous grin on his face, though his small, pale lips were pursed and shut. Everyone, however, was not standing, and among the sitters he saw Pinel, arms folded. As the applause subsided, De Gerando began to speak. Dear De Gerando!

"Citizen Itard, your report bears overwhelming witness to your extraordinary success, but I must add that I have been fortunate in actually *seeing* the fruits of your patience, perception, and genius. Yes, genius!—in the devising of unique and unprecedented tools and techniques for drawing the civilized from the savage, and advancing our understanding of humankind. I have no doubts that we may anticipate, based on what, in this brief time, you have already achieved, a great deal more from this experiment. My dear friend: Bravo! And bravo again!"

De Gerando sat, hands went up, and Pinel's was the one that caught Itard's eye. His chest tightened as he nodded to his former professor. Pinel rose, folded his arms, and gazed at the chandelier.

"I, too, offer my congratulations. Some of your techniques are quite interesting, and the very fact of your undertaking such a doubtful task is . . . laudable. But what you have actually accomplished and what final conclusions we may reach, I think, remain to be seen. And I heard nothing in your report that contradicts my original diagnosis of idiocy. If you have devised means for diminishing the child's wildness, it only implies that he was a social being before his life in the wild, and you were able to remind him of it. My ultimate prognosis remains a bleak one; you have accomplished all you shall."

Abbé Sicard spoke from his place at the front, beside Itard.

"Yes, Citizen Pinel, I must say I agree. What Itard has done is admirable, and we applaud his efforts, but I have seen the boy—what do you call him? Victor? He is clean, you have dressed him; he does not mess the floor or his bed, and it is now *more* evident that he is not a normal child but an idiot, as I have always known."

"Citizen Sicard—" It was the astronomer, Lalande, rising to his feet. "I will not dispute your expertise—or Citizen Pinel's—when it comes to idiocy. Even in a republic there are, unfortunately, abundant examples. But what Citizen Itard has accomplished makes the point *meaningless*, don't you think? That this young man stepped in where experts twice his age threw up their hands, and did what he has done—I am very impressed! This report should be published, and I look forward to further developments with great interest."

There was a scatter of affirming applause and another hand rose.

"Citizen Itard, why did you not bring the boy so that we might all see and evaluate his progress for ourselves?"

"Ever since his capture, he has been stared at, poked, and studied—on display like something in a zoo. This, I am convinced, exacerbated his dehumanization, and much of my effort went to counteracting just this treatment. He is not yet ready for renewed display, but if any of you, individually, would like to meet him, you are most welcome to come and visit."

Dr. Virey, the noted naturalist, raised his hand.

"Citizen, do you have a specific plan for the next phase of your work with the child?"

"I do!" Itard was startled at his own assurance. "I am going to continue along the path mapped by Condillac. The intellect is reached through the senses. I will continue working to develop each of them in turn. The first will be hearing."

"But you say his hearing is good."

"Yes, it's acute when it pertains to his needs or survival,

but he has not yet learned to *listen*—to truly distinguish one sound from another. This will be my first goal. Then sight—*seeing*. He has begun to see and recognize words; we shall continue in that direction. Then, I'll do more work with touch. Taste and smell, of course, are less connected to the intellect, but I have seen that they can be used to reach it. And, finally, the intellect itself; memory and reason and the communication of ideas, which will lead, ultimately, to *speech*."

"The next report," interjected De Gerando, "will be given by Victor himself."

"What is the nature of his interaction with other children?" It was someone in the rear; Itard couldn't remember the name. "Does he play with them?"

"When he first came to the Institute, he suffered a good deal of abuse at the hands of the boys there, and he's understandably fearful and mistrustful of children. In addition, I've been concerned that their muteness might reinforce his own; for these reasons, I've kept his contact with them to a minimum."

Itard nodded to the hand of a man he knew to be an eminent physician.

"Citizen Itard, what are the manifestations of this 'explosive puberty,' and how will you deal with them?"

Itard took a breath. "I . . . really cannot say more at this time. Decency does not allow—permit—uh, specifics. There is absolutely no doubt that it is puberty we are dealing with, and in its . . . rawest form. There is no social veneer to mask the true nature of this process, and . . . really, I cannot say more, but to assure you that I will present everything in future reports, no matter how . . . disturbing they may prove."

"And your methods for dealing with this puberty?" It was Lalande. "Can you give us some hints?"

"I . . . am trying various . . . approaches. I can say no more. Again, I thank you all for this opportunity."

"Well done! Well done!" Jauffret and Cuvier were smiling at him. There was more applause, and then he was surrounded with smiles—someone was slapping him on the back—and hands grasped his with heartiest congratulations and earnest expressions of interest in one or another aspect of his work. "We shall publish it! Oh, yes, the world must know of this!"

Enough! Limp and spent, Itard was longing to be home, longing to be alone.

24

10 Nivôse, Year X
(January 1, 1802)

This evening, Victor and I celebrated our first anniversary; also present were Madame and Monsieur Guérin, Julie, and a marvelous cake, which Victor, of course, would not touch, preferring instead an extra serving of his beloved lentils. He still finds sweets repulsive; this year, perhaps, we shall see that change. Tomorrow we begin work on hearing. What new discoveries and accomplishments await us in our second year?

On the table there are things.
There are bells. There is Victor's drum and a drum that is not Victor's.
There are sticks.
"Look, Victor; this is my bell and this is yours—no!—leave it on the table; we'll ring them soon enough. And the drums—these are your sticks, and these are mine. Here's my old scarf, the one you like the feel of. My

mother sent it to me long ago. It's very soft, isn't it?"

The doctor brings the scarf over Victor's face. The world disappears. There is darkness and Victor watches the flashes. They float this way and that. They come and go. The scarf lowers. Here is the table, the drums, the bells, the world.

"You're like a baby playing peekaboo, Victor. Did anyone ever play that with you? First you see them, then you *hear* them—it's a *listening* game, Victor. Please let me know if the scarf is too tight."

The scarf is all around his head, and so is darkness, dust, sweat, and chalk. The doctor smell. Victor turns his head this way and it's the same; and the same this way; and this way also. He watches the flashes.

"Listen, Victor. *Listen.* What do you hear?"

The doctor is doing something. Something.

"Listen, Victor, can you make this sound?"

Hands put something in his hand. Something hard. Cold. The hand moves his hand. A bell! He shakes it. He holds it up close to the scarf and sniffs: metal and wood.

"Yes, Victor! That is your bell."

Victor shakes his bell.

"Very good, Victor. *Listen.* What do you hear now? No, it's not a bell. Listen . . ." Hands take Victor's hand. The hands give him something. Sticks.

"Listen, Victor."

The hands raise his hand, and then lower it. Drum! Drum again! Victor laughs. Drum! Drum again!

"Do as I do. What do you hear? Yes! The bell! Ring your bell! Good! And now? No, that's not the bell. Listen.

174

What's in your other hand? The drumstick! Listen and do as I do. Yes! The drum!"

In the darkness he hears a drum. He swings his stick. Victor's drum! He hears a bell. He shakes his bell. Bell again! Victor's bell!

"Good, Victor—now listen. Put down your bell and take this. Strike it with your stick. This is not a drum. Listen. It's the coal shovel! Listen."

Victor hears the stick strike the coal shovel. He swings his stick and hears it again. He laughs and hears his laugh. He hears the bell. He rings his bell. He hears the drum. He strikes his drum. He hears the shovel. He strikes and hears it again. He hears the doctor speaking.

"You're good at this game, Victor! Excellent!"

He feels the doctor's enormous hand on his neck. The doctor's fingers on his neck in the darkness and the flashes are everywhere. He hears Victor laughing, and in the darkness, deep in the darkness there is something. Victor reaches down with his hands to find it, down into the darkness—there is something. Something. He must find it. It will not go away . . .

"No, Victor! You know we don't do that! Take the bell. Here, take the drumstick. Listen, Victor! *Listen!*"

9 *Ventôse, Year X*
(February 28, 1802)

Itard opened the door to his study and looked in. Victor knelt, silhouetted in front of the window, his face turned up to a dove-gray sky; snowflakes clicked softly at the panes. The boy's body gyrated around and back and forth. His hands were hidden but Itard could see the elbows pumping, and he heard the soft grunt, as of annoyance, repeated over and over.

"Victor." The boy froze. "It's time for the scarf."

Without looking around, Victor scrambled across the room to the bureau and pulled open the bottom drawer. He snatched up the old gray woolen scarf, and ran with it to Itard. Trembling and squirming, he tried to hold still while it was wrapped around his head.

"Calm, Victor . . . calm. We've been doing this for two months; why does it still delight you so? It's excessive! You must be calm or we can't play. Here—here is the table; sit here. Calmly!"

Victor wagged his head and giggled. After almost two months, blindfolded as many as three hours a day, Victor could tell immediately—by the sound—a drum's rim from its side, a large glass from a small, or a wooden block from a box, and he could respond with a like sound. Confident that this first step was well accomplished three weeks ago, Itard had introduced vocal sounds: at first loud, simple consonants, then progressively softer and more subtle ones. And then the vowels.

"These are the beginnings of speech!" he had told the boy, and felt a tremor of excitement and awe at reaching this longed-for moment. "Speech: the almost God-like power that gives form and substance to thought, and to man his supremacy. Once you can hear and differentiate the vowels, Victor, the road to speech is clear . . ."

After the months of drums and bells and shovels, Victor responded to the voice with a delight that seemed to confirm all of Itard's hopes. He began pursuing Itard with the scarf between lessons, tugging at him and begging for the game. But, day by day, his joyous enthusiasm grew more disruptive, frenzied, and hysterical.

Now, half his face obscured by the scarf, Victor sat like some entranced, turbaned magician, mouth open, tongue wagging back and forth, his whole body vibrating in anticipation.

Since Victor was as yet incapable of imitating the sounds, Itard had tried to have him raise a different finger to acknowledge each one.

"You remember what we did yesterday? You hold up your thumb when you hear A." Victor bounced and hummed. "You lift this finger for E." Victor panted and squealed. "The third one for I . . . the fourth is O, and the little one is U." The table and chair rocked and saliva flew from Victor's mouth as his head whipped back and forth.

"Calm, Victor . . . calm." This brought a rapturous screech.

"We'll begin with *eeeee* . . ." said Itard softly, and tapped the boy's index finger. There was a screech of high-pitched laughter. The finger didn't move.

"*Eeeeee* . . ." Itard repeated. Screeches and table pounding.

Itard made his voice stern, laden with warning. Gentleness and patience were no longer productive.

"Victor, no more! You must stop this!" The boy giggled. Faint *oooo*'s and barely expressed *ahhhh*'s set him quivering. At certain sounds—a soft *uuuu*—he shrieked and slipped his hands under the table to search and rub until Itard pulled them away. The morning was passing as had the one yesterday and the one before. And the one before. What to do, what to do? Something drastic.

Itard's arm shot across the table and yanked away the scarf.

"Enough!" he shouted, half out of his chair and glaring. "This cannot go on! You will *not* ruin our work. *You will not!* You understand perfectly, don't you?"

Victor looked startled: at the sudden light, at the angry face. Then he laughed and bounced.

"*Victor!*" The boy's face melted into uncertainty. "I warn you . . ." Victor squeezed his eyes shut and slipped his hands under the table. He began to giggle and rock.

Itard's fist slammed the table inches from the child's face. "*No! No! No!*" Victor's eyes popped open. Terror. His head turned this way and that; seeing the scarf on the floor, he jumped up, snatched it, and ran crowing to Itard with it, wrapping it around his own eyes.

"My God, it's no good! It's no good!" Itard pressed his own face into his hands and rubbed his eyes and forehead. "A useful tool has become a meaningless game—and we are so close! Whatever you learn, Victor—every step forward—you use to thwart me! No more! No more scarf, Victor. It's finished." He tossed the scarf into the drawer and locked it. Victor scurried after him, mewing.

"Sit down now, come . . . We will work without it." He pressed the boy back into his chair, and resumed his own place opposite. Anger clenched his jaw and Victor looked apprehensive. Good. I'll gnash my teeth a bit. Good.

"All right. We will begin . . . again. Look here at me. Listen: *uuuuu* . . ."

Ventôse 16

Victor's gaze drifted through the room.

"*Uuuuu*, Victor . . . look here; *uuuuuu!* . . ."

Victor's eyes seemed to follow the slow, erratic course of some invisible flying insect.

"Look *here*, Victor! *Uuuuuu!*"

Victor clamped his hands between his thighs and began to rock. Motes of dust took his attention, first one, then another.

Then another.

Ventôse 17

"Victor, is this the end? Is this as far as you come to meet me? Halfway out of the forest, Victor? Will you never speak to me?"

Victor's mouth hung open. He stared at the window and rocked. Itard turned to the window. More snow. At home, except for the dazzle that capped the distant peaks, snow was rare. He'd never had his fill of it: watching it, being in it.

"Shall we play in the snow, Victor? Let it go for today? Will tomorrow be different?" Victor rocked and rubbed. Itard sat. The clock chipped away at the afternoon. What to do?

Ventôse 21

Itard sighed.

"All right, Victor, we'll try the scarf once more. Once more . . . you're quiet now; stay quiet. I'll get it."

At the sight of it, Victor's eyes shone. When it was round his head, he bounced and slapped the table.

"No, Victor!" Itard picked up a drumstick and rapped his knuckles. Victor flinched. Then he crowed and held his hand out again.

"It's not a *game*, damn you!" Itard shouted and struck the knuckles more sharply.

Victor froze, his tongue poised in the middle of his open mouth. He began to quiver. A tear crept from under the scarf and meandered down his face. Others silently followed, dripping from his chin onto the table. Hesitantly, Itard removed the scarf. The boy's eyes were squeezed shut and, except for a slight trembling and the continuing tears, he didn't move.

"Oh God, *enough*! Why must I *do* this? Why do I spend my days tormenting a demented child?" Itard collapsed forward in his chair, pressed his face into his hands, and rocked back and forth. "Victor, Victor! I wish to God I'd never laid eyes on you! It is *cruel*! You don't belong here—

here in this stinking world! You were complete! You were whole—you needed nothing—felt no pain—knew *nothing*! And now I've made you like us—like me! Needing, needing, *needing*! Clothes, houses, chairs, tables, rugs, vases . . . Dining out! All this trash! And worst of all, needing the praise and love and approval of your fellow citizens—the cruelest, stupidest animals in creation! What have I done to you? Go back to the goddamned *woods*! We'll go together; you can teach me!"

Itard sat up and gathered the limp, broken boy into his arms, pressed him to his chest and rocked harder. "Ah, Victor, Victor, I'm so tired. A whole year—more!—to come to this! What made me think I could do it? What am I doing wrong?"

Itard found himself sobbing, his mouth twisted into a knot, his own huge tears blinding him.

"I am so tired. I'm young! What kind of a life is this? I'm cloistered here in this prison, day and night with you—all these children who neither hear nor speak. A woman . . . I should be married—where is my wife? I need to go south, home to my hills, my mountains . . . I'll get some goats! We'll be goatherds, Victor, you and I. That's exactly what we'll do! We'll live in the hills with the goats and learn their language; we'll read the stars . . . Oh God, I'm tired . . . so tired."

25

From time to time, as she walks, she opens her closed fist and looks to make sure of the scrap of paper, now damp, on which the doctor scrawled the address: 74. What will it be like? Who will be there? She walks along the quays and breathes the river smell, watery and enormous: the green-brown smell of things growing and rotting and dissolving into the rippling, muscular river to grow and rot again. The smell of spring. Countless barges slide past, all floating under the shouts and laughter of the bargemen; this one piled high with wine barrels, that one with lumber, another crammed with pigs, another full of bleating sheep who, like me, thinks Julie, don't know where they're going.

This is the part of the river she loves best, but only rarely has she walked here—past these palaces and then over the bridge to a world of fine houses, and Notre Dame rising up like heaven itself.

The doctor said I will like them, but will they like me? What if it's awful? What if there's someone like Nicholas? Most of the people walking here are women: servants and housekeepers. She looks at them, but they don't look at her, even the ones that still have country clothes and complexions; they are too taken up with their errands, their packages and baskets. Her basket holds everything. All her clothes, her comb and brush, and Clothilde, her old rag doll. Eyes lowered, she passes the men. They *all* look at her: carpenters, housepainters, even delivery boys and filthy chimney sweeps with their brooms. Some of them say things she pretends not to hear.

Nicholas! Even now she feels the tears brim. Rage and pain . . . how could he be so sweet and so awful? So vile! After Evelyn had caught him with Julie, she'd made a point of never leaving them alone together. Nicholas still teased her and made her blush with secret blown kisses and obscene gestures from across the room, but except for an occasional stolen pinch or poke, he almost never touched her, and life had returned to the usual drudgery until Rose began throwing up her breakfast. After a week of it, Evelyn cornered her and wouldn't let her go till she began to cry and told everything: how she and Nicholas . . . The thought of it *still* made Julie want to double over. Another baby! Rose's baby—*her* little Nicholas!

She had heard that her father, when he was told, jumped out of bed shouting he was going to get his pick and kill that son of a bitch, until he collapsed, barely able to breathe. But her mother, who had always been crazy about

Nicholas, marched across Paris, burst into the house, and slapped his face again and again, shouting things that made Julie's hair stand on end. Evelyn applauded her mother and urged her on while Rose wailed and wept and Julie huddled in the corner holding poor, frightened little Albert, who whimpered for his mama.

"Julie!" Her mother had suddenly turned to her. "Get your things! You're not staying here another minute with this . . . this *creature!*"

"I can live with you and Papa?" Julie's heart rose up.

"No, of course not! You know that's not possible. You'll stay with us a few days till we find you a suitable place— somewhere you can earn your keep." Julie's heart sank into her belly. What would it be? Where would it be? Would she ever see her mother and father? Her sisters?

74. Julie compares the brass numerals to the scrawl on her paper. They match. Her stomach twists like a wrung-out washrag as she goes up the marble steps. The knocker is brass and huge. She looks at it for a while. Then, with both hands, she lifts and drops it twice before she notices a bell pull and is overwhelmed with panic—should she have used that instead?

The door opens. There is a tall woman in a blue silk dress of the kind on which she and her sisters sew seams, hems, and buttonholes.

"You must be Julie." The woman smiles. "I am Madame De Gerando. Come in. Doctor Itard has spoken so well of you."

The hall is cool and smells of wax. She follows the

woman past chairs and tables that glow softly in the lace-filtered light. The green carpet is thick and springy, like the new grass in the Luxembourg Gardens.

"Please, sit." The woman waves Julie to a striped silk couch. "Jean-Marc . . . the doctor has told me that besides being a fine seamstress and an excellent cook, you are very pleasant and good-natured—like your mother, whom he also often praises. He's told us how marvelous she's been with Victor. She is a very remarkable woman, isn't she?"

"Yes, Madame." Julie stares down at her own cracked black shoes, which had also been her sister's. Madame De Gerando goes on to tell her what her duties will be: the washing and ironing, the floors, the dusting and the marketing, as well as the cooking. Julie studies the flowers and birds woven into the carpet and from time to time she nods and mumbles, "Yes, Madame."

"Is there anything you would like to ask me?" says Madame De Gerando. "Any questions?"

Julie, eyes still on the carpet, shakes her head.

"Very well, then." Madame De Gerando stands and so does Julie. "I know I shall be very pleased with you and, as time goes on, I hope you are less shy and come to confide in me. You will find me to be sympathetic and fair. I see you've brought your things; you can begin right away. Do you read or write?" Julie glances up.

"A little, Madame. I once made an alphabet. I can make some words . . ." She looks down.

"You've made your own alphabet?"

"Yes, Madame. Once. From cut paper."

"Well, Julie, if you like, I will teach you to read—and to write as well. Writing is very useful. Would you like that?"

"Yes, Madame."

"Good. I would enjoy it also. We can spend an hour every afternoon. Come, I'll show you your room."

Julie follows up the stairs. Step by step she feels she is walking into the sky.

26

3 *Prairial, Year X*
(May 23, 1802)

An extraordinary event! It happened today during the demonstration of a new instrument that, according to its inventor, produces sounds that can penetrate even the ears of the deaf. The sounds were piercing indeed, and most of the boys Sicard had selected for the demonstration *seemed* to hear them. Suspecting they might be shamming, it then occurred to me to suggest blindfolding some of them and trying the experiment again. My suspicions were confirmed; none of them responded at first. But with repeated tries, more and more *did* hear the sounds!

Like a bolt of lightning, it struck me—this was a technique to teach the deaf to hear! I then described to Sicard the sound training I'd done with Victor, and he couldn't conceal his enthusiasm. (It seems, also, that the attention resulting from the publication of my report has enhanced his regard for my efforts.) Beginning next week, at his insistence, I will work regularly with a group of deaf children to enhance their hearing.

If nothing further were to come of my struggle to have Victor speak, this would be adequate reward and affirmation. But more will come, I'm sure of it, and progress has been made; Victor's understanding now encompasses many more words, and he's become sensitive to the slightest intonation of emotion in my voice. Nevertheless, I must now admit that in the two months since the disruptive gaiety vanished with the rapping of his knuckles, we've been at an almost total impasse. The fearfulness that has replaced the hysteria is no more productive. Today it took fifteen long minutes of gentle, patient urging before Victor, with painful uncertainty, responded to a single sound. Now he seems terrified of making mistakes. Had the fearfulness been there all along, masked by the roisterous behavior? Or is it purely the result of the knuckle rapping, and the rebuke it represented? His emotional sensibilities are indeed fully developed. I must continue to be careful of them, and use them always to our advantage. I push all doubts aside. Victor will speak.

In any case, I shall suspend the sound training for now and go on to sight. The change should be welcome and refreshing for both of us.

The doctor taps and screeches the chalk across the slate. Look here, Victor. What have we here?

Victor taps his chalk on his slate but there are no

screeches. He taps harder. No, Victor! It's writing. See the marks? Look here!

The doctor taps at Victor's slate. There are screeches and Victor smells the chalk and in the light he sees the chalk-snow, falling and floating over the doctor's black jacket and trousers. He smells the doctor and the doctor's shirt. He touches the doctor's jacket and trousers. There is something. He can't find it. There is something.

Victor, no! Stop now, and look here. Look here, Victor.

1 Vendémiaire, XI
(September 23, 1802)

It has been exactly four months since we began concentrating on sight. Today, without fail, when I pointed to a word in the list on my slate, Victor, at a glance, found it on his. Not only had I jumbled their order, but I had added words to his list that did not appear on mine. He has also begun to write! The hours and hours—the months—at the blackboard teaching him to imitate: do as I do, mark as I mark—bear fruit at last! Today I pointed to the word *eau* and he reproduced it—crudely, but legibly! I conclude from this that he sees the word as I do, though nothing can be taken for granted. It might mean something very different. Words are still meaningless symbols that he neither understands nor pronounces, but I am convinced that attaching objects and sounds to them will not be as difficult as what we have already achieved.

Meanwhile, the parade of patients that continues to besiege me is astounding; most come for hearing difficulties, but there are those with other complaints as well. I have accepted three more into my private practice and have decided that two mornings a week will be the full extent of it for now. The work with the deaf children is also going very well. Very gratifying. Whatever the causes of deafness, it seems sure that they cannot be seen; the dissections I've done on cadavers of the deaf, though fascinating, reveal no visible abnormality.

Victor, however, remains my first priority. Tomorrow, along with continuing the work with words and writing, I intend to try an idea I've had: to refine, and use, his sense of touch.

Look into the vase.

Darkness. The doctor's vase.

There are things. He can smell them. There is an acorn. There is metal. Cut metal. Is there stone? Victor reaches his hand into the darkness. Deeper and deeper it goes until it is gone.

"What is in the vase, Victor? Can you find a stone like this one?" The doctor holds a stone and Victor's fingers search the darkness. Like a forest, reaching under a tree, searching among the roots. Grubs. Juicy beetles. He touches something. Paper. This is a button and this—*yes!* This is a stone. The doctor holds a stone in his hand and Victor's hand comes up out of the darkness, out of the vase and—*yes!* He has a stone. He sniffs it. It smells of stone and the vase. It smells of the doctor.

"Good boy, Victor!"

22 Vendémiaire, XI
(October 14, 1802)

Victor's work with the vase has been effective beyond my hopes. Today, unerringly, he found in it the mate for every cutout letter I showed him. Even finding G among C, O, and Q gave him no difficulty. His sense of touch is more than adequate, and I am confident that he is ready for the next phase, though I'll continue to use these exercises for their calming effect. Somehow they free him, for a while, from the torments of puberty; his face at peace, and the profound thoughtfulness in his eyes as his fingers search the vase—I never tire of watching it.

I took on another new patient today—a Polish count. He seemed in such distress and had come so far, I couldn't turn him away. Every day, I turn away at least two, some days more. It seems that, what with Victor and the deaf children, my research and writing, and my practice, which grows in spite of my best efforts to limit it, the days grow, each one, a little longer, a little deeper into the night. And yet I am never tired and I have never been happier. Even so, it's after three; to bed!

He dreams he's making his way down a narrow street.

His progress is slow because of piles of rubbish: broken chairs, tables, and other furniture, as well as pieces of crockery, rotting vegetables, and even chunks of meat. As he goes, he has to put these piles into some order. In one, there is a dead dog and the corpse of a baby. In another, there are human heads that have to be arranged in a particular way in relation to the other debris. What a revolting job, he thinks to himself, and yet he goes about it conscientiously, as he does everything. A scarf is wrapped around the lower part of his face and over his nose so as to block the stench—which it does—for he notices none. His mother, however, *does* notice; she is with him, clutching his arm and complaining bitterly about being subjected to these horrors. He realizes then that he is looking for Victor. I must find him, he tells his mother. He feels a surge of panic. Perhaps the boy is lost for good; perhaps he's dead. Itard is startled to realize that he has no trousers on, but, fortunately, his mother is so taken up with her complaints that she doesn't notice. A low fog that obscures the tops of the buildings suddenly lifts and reveals sumptuous green hills littered with tremendous orange pumpkins, some large as a house. The sight fills him with joy and he points it out to his mother, and then sees Victor, running naked up the hill among the pumpkins. Itard calls to him, and the boy turns and runs back down. As he approaches, Itard sees that he is now nicely dressed, with his hair neatly combed.

"I have to go home now," says Victor, in his lovely bell-like voice. His French is flawless. "The Abbé Sicard has taught me to speak and now I am writing a philosophical history of the universe." He is indeed writing, and has covered what seems to be hundreds of pages in a beautiful hand.

"But, Victor," says Itard, "what shall I do now?"

Then he's awake.

27

2 *Brumaire, Year XI*
(October 24, 1803)

"Here is the list, Victor. Please bring me these things."

Itard held up the slate, and Victor's eyes, blinking rapidly, flitted back and forth over the carefully chalked words:

BOOK

KNIFE

CUP

TONGS

SCISSORS

BRUSH

PEN

He then slipped his arm through the basket handle and trotted out of the doctor's study, down the hall toward his room.

Itard saw him pause, as always, at the tall window that looked toward the hills. The sight of sky, especially moving clouds in changing light, *still* arrested him! He stood staring, and the sound he made—a kind of mewing—was it wonder? Joy? Longing? The autumn sun silvered his profile and illuminated the pupils of his eyes.

Beautiful, murmured Itard.

"Yes, Victor, it's beautiful—but go on now! The list—don't forget the list." But Victor no longer forgot. How long had it been? Itard searched quickly back through his journal. My God! It's been another year.

Itard had waited, despite his ache to begin this phase—attaching words to objects and expanding the memory—until he was absolutely sure Victor was ready. When that day came, Itard had set on a shelf those same familiar objects: the brush, the cup, the pen, the tongs, the knife, each with its name printed on a card. Then he separated name from object and Victor had to reunite them, again and again till, in his heart and mind, each word and thing were married.

Once again, progress had seemed agonizingly slow. But it came. And then Itard showed Victor a word and had him fetch the object it referred to from across the room. At first, the word had to be in sight constantly, but after several weeks, a glance was enough, and then Itard began to add things: the cup and the knife; the cup and the knife and the book; the book and the pen and the tongs and the knife . . . My God, what a *struggle*! Each day deciding to abandon the whole damn thing and each day beginning again. Beginning again and again. And so, as the months passed,

Victor's memory expanded to contain more and more words, and then they began to stretch it over space and time. Now, after showing him a list, Itard sent him down the hall to fetch the things from his room. At first, Victor ran, trying to outrace his brief memory, and failed, and returned to the list again and again. And again.

All those months of persistence and patience, never having dreamed such patience existed, and all the while struggling with that . . . relentless puberty.

From across the apartment, Itard heard the door open and close, the quick small steps in the hall and, again, the pause at the window. The clock ticked off a minute and then Victor was at the desk, carefully laying before the doctor the tongs, the cup, the knife, the scissors, the brush, the pen, the book. Itard held up the list and they both checked it off: objects and symbols of objects. Words, too, are objects, and proof of those invisible creations of the invisible mind: ideas. Are there ideas, Victor, without words? What might they be?

"Excellent, Victor! Everything is here. Everything. I am very pleased and very proud. I can see that you are pleased because I am pleased—but you should be *proud* also. We must teach you pride and we must decide how to proceed from here. Yes, we are going on, Victor! You are an excellent boy! Come, let's celebrate with a cup of milk."

Victor snatched up his cup and slipped it into his pocket, and Itard was chilled by a subtle twist of misgiving. His satisfaction evaporated. What was it?

"No, Victor, leave that here, the kitchen is full of cups.

Let's drink from a different one today." He tried to take the cup, but Victor clasped it to his chest and avoided the doctor's eyes.

"All right, then, bring it. Yes, it's your cup, Victor's cup."

Victor galloped ahead, cup held before him in both hands. Bringing the slate and the chalk, Itard locked the door behind them and overtook Victor in front of the cupboard. He was trotting in place, turning circles, his cup clasped to his lips. Itard thought of this as his milk dance.

"Will there come a day when you no longer do this, Victor? Other boys don't, you know, even deaf ones; they stand patiently and wait. Will you always be part puppy, Victor?"

As the milk was poured, Victor was absolutely still, and then, with the same attention, he drank.

"Other boys. There are some nice ones, you know. I've thought it might be time to have you play with one or two who can speak a bit—you shall speak, too—but there's your damn puberty. I don't know how they'd react to all that . . . It might be upsetting to them, as it was to Julie— though more likely they'd laugh, and I won't have you laughed at. We shall see . . ."

"*Lait,*" said Victor when his cup was empty. "*Lait.*" He licked his lips clean.

"Yes, milk, my boy. *Lait.* It was good. Now, shall we work a bit more? Look here—what am I writing on the slate? Knife, bowl, tongs, spoon." Itard waved to the shelves and cupboard. "They are all here in the kitchen. Please bring them to me."

Victor scanned the slate and then ran from the room. Itard heard Victor's gallop echo through the hall to the door of his study, then the rattle of the locked latch. There was a pause and the shoes clattered back and Victor was there, urgently tugging at Itard's sleeve and patting the pocket where he kept his keys.

"No, no, Victor, we don't need to unlock the study. Look! Here in the kitchen—we have a knife—we have bowls— we have tongs. Bring me one of these." As he peered at the doctor's face, Victor's eyes went blank. His hands slid between his thighs and he began rocking back and forth. The fear that had been nibbling at Itard's hopes suddenly swallowed them.

"No, Victor . . ." Itard took the boy firmly by the wrists and gave him the slate. "Look! The knife." He underlined the word with his finger and then picked up the thing that Madame Guérin used to cut bread. "It's here! *This* is a knife! *This* is a bowl! *These* are tongs!" Itard lined them up on the table. Victor stood looking from slate to table to doctor and back again.

"Please, Victor—how can you not understand? Please bring me the knife, the bowl . . ." Itard heard himself pleading, and Victor was gone again, clattering down the hall to the study, pausing at the view, and rattling once again at the locked door. Itard slumped into a chair, doubled over by the full realization that Victor did not know what a knife was—or a bowl, or tongs, or a shirt, or a pen— or any of the things he had words for. Only the knife in the study was a "knife." The one in the kitchen was some *other* thing, and there were no bowls here, no spoons—only the things in the study were "bowls" and "spoons." Victor tugged at the doctor's sleeve, patted his pocket.

"Don't you *see* this is a bowl? Don't you *see* these are tongs? You *are* an idiot! An *idiot*! All my patience and my cunning and care—my *life*! Wasted on an idiot! Look! It's a knife! It cuts the bread! Don't you see, damn you? Don't you see?"

He gripped Victor's arms and shouted into his uncomprehending face.

"Back to the woods! Go back to the goddamned woods! I don't want to see you again! Ever! Go to the woods and die there—or Bicêtre! Yes, now that I've spent two, almost *three* years making you an idiot—with all my heart and sweat and hope—you can go and die in Bicêtre with all the other *idiots*!"

He shoved the boy against a chair and it fell and Victor bumped the shelves; a cup smashed on the floor. The boy's chest and belly began to spasm with sobs. A line of blood-streaked snot slid from his nose, and the tears began. From his twisted mouth came a rattling squeal. He slid his hands deep into his pants, bent completely over, and stood rocking and squealing.

"Yes, howl, damn you! I'm finished with you! I am not an idiot! I am a doctor! People come from all over the world to see me! I teach the deaf to speak! I can teach stones to speak! But not *idiots*!"

Itard stared out the window into the smoky haze over the city. He shivered from the sweat that chilled his neck and armpits, and as rage drained away he was left with the simple clarity of the truth.

The fault was his. He was the teacher. Because they had worked *only* with the things in his study, he had spent months teaching Victor that *only* those things belonged to the words. Victor had learned what he'd been taught. His understanding was perfect, and perfectly transparent. It was the teacher that hadn't understood his own lessons.

The boy's body and face were twisted and distorted by a pain so primal that Itard winced.

"Oh, no, no, Victor . . ." He knelt by the boy. He wrapped his arms around him and began to rock with him.

"I'm sorry, I'm so sorry, so sorry—you are a good boy, a good boy—you are not an idiot—I am the idiot. You are Victor . . . Victor, and we will begin again . . . begin again . . ."

28

"And . . . she . . . watched as . . . the face . . . of the . . . Beast was . . . transformed . . . into that . . . of a . . . young and . . . handsome . . . prince . . ."

Julie's finger moves from one clump of letters to the next, and each blossoms into a word, and then a picture, and she sees it all: Beauty weeping in the shadowy garden. She even smells the roses, hears the Beast's last, rasping breaths—and then witnesses the miraculous transformation. Julie weeps also. Although a handsome prince is a wonderful thing, she, too, had come to love the Beast. She reads the last word on the last page, Beauty and the prince are married and the two jealous sisters have turned to stone. She closes the book and stares at it. All she just experienced is contained in the thing she holds in her hand.

She looks around the room. The walls are full of books. Madame De Gerando has shown her a few of them. Some have pictures of places she's never dreamed of, some have charts that show all the countries of the world. Some are in other languages, made of other alphabets. All of them, thinks Julie, I will read all of them.

"Did you finish it, Julie?" Madame De Gerando comes into the library.

"Yes, Madame."

"Did you enjoy it?"

"Oh, yes, Madame!"

"Good! Maybe, soon, you can write one like it."

"I? I . . . don't know any stories, Madame . . ."

Madame De Gerando laughs. "Of course you do. Everyone knows stories. But until you begin to write, you can't really know *what* you know. Let's do some more writing. Open your pad, take your pen and ink, and write something about yourself. Anything that comes to mind."

Julie carefully dips her pen. For a moment she looks out the window at the sky. A sparrow flies past. Then, very carefully, moving the pen across the paper, leaving a trail of loops and curves, dots and lines, she writes:

My name is Julie Guérin. I am happy.

29

Degerando degerando degerando . . .

Over and over he hears it in the rattles and creaks of the carriage, the jangling trappings of the horses and the clatter of their hooves: degerando degerando . . . And he can see lentils steaming and sausage steaming and he can smell them and the beans and the chicken; they are not here in the carriage but soon he will have them, soon it will stop being carriage and be degerando degerando degerando . . .

Now it's street! Now it's door! Degerando!

"Victor! It's been so long—look how you've grown! And Jean-Marc! My dear friend, congratulations! Here we've finally gotten you and Adèle together and we weren't sure you'd be coming. We thought you might already be on your way to Saint Petersburg! Coats, hats, walking stick—come in! Come in!"

Yes, smell the lentils degerando! Yes, sausage. Yes, beans. Yes, degerando!

"Jean-Marc, this—at long last—is my niece Adèle, whose virtues and charms I might have mentioned to you. I confess, Adèle, I brag of you shamelessly and endlessly. And, Adèle, this is my dear friend Jean-Marc, the famous Citizen Doctor Itard, of whom you've heard at least as much. And, evidently, the czar of Russia has heard of him also—though not from me—and wants to steal him from us. Of course, we won't allow it. And, of course, this is Victor. Did the czar invite you also, Victor? He'll want to sniff your hand, Adèle."

Flowers and vinegar and rice powder. Warm and wet. Noisy clothes.

"Enough, Victor! Stop now. I've looked forward to meeting you, Adèle. I hope Victor doesn't upset you—he's not always quite so . . . excited. I wasn't going to bring him, but his governess is away with her husband, who is gravely ill. Coming here always excites Victor, anyway: his favorite foods, and, of course, a new person . . ."

Degerando! Degerando! Madame Degerando!

"My dear Victor! Hello, hello!" Almonds and sausage and flowers and sausage . . . "Jean-Marc, my dear, is it true? You cannot go! We won't allow it! Come in! Do you like my dress, Victor? It smells good, does it? You may hug me . . . He likes to hug, and to pat also, yes, you may pat, but gently . . . No, no, gently! . . . on my arms. Go on to the kitchen now, someone needs your help."

Degerando degerando, kitchen degerando . . . Julie!

"Hello, Victor. How are you? Hungry as usual, I see . . .
Good! Come, take these plates and bowls. First we'll set the
table, and then we'll bring in the casseroles."

Lentils Julie! Plates Julie! Beans and spoons Julie!
Degerando Julie! Degerando plates! Sniff the plates,
smooth and shiny. Big plates degerando. Big bowls
degerando. One two three. One two three degerando!

"Good evening, Julie," said Itard. "I see you've put Victor
to work. How are you?"

"I'm well, thank you, Doctor." She set down the platter
and curtsied. "How is my father?"

"We've done all we can. He's very weak, I'm afraid.
Very weak. Your mother is with him at your sister's
house."

"After dinner," said Madame De Gerando, "you may go
and join them."

"Thank you, Madame." Julie hurried back to the
kitchen, Victor close behind her.

"He's dying," said Itard.

Madame De Gerando nodded. "I know. Poor Julie. She
does her work and shows almost nothing, but I hear her,
sometimes, weeping in the kitchen, or while she's making
the beds. It's so sad. What about Victor? Does he know?
Does he understand?"

"No." Itard shook his head. "He knows something is
going on; it's in the air—but not death. Not yet. He understands only what he sees and touches."

They looked into the fireplace and watched the fire for a

moment. It collapsed and Itard glanced up at Adèle. She stood quietly to his right. She smiled. Her resemblance to De Gerando startled him.

"Your uncle tells me," said Itard, "that, like me, you are a tutor . . . English children, is it? How old are they?"

"Oh, a tutor, yes, but not like you . . ." Her smile was disconcerting; De Gerando with freckles. "I simply teach French to three normal children. The girls are eight and ten, and little Robert, their brother, is almost five. I teach them French and they teach me English—very different from what you do."

"Not really. I've been teaching French to Victor for years—he's learning, though he doesn't speak—and Victor teaches me all kinds of things."

Julie reappeared with another platter, and Victor trotted behind with a stack of dinner plates and began meticulously arranging the table.

"What does he teach you," said Adèle, "may I ask?"

Itard tried to reconcile her with the person De Gerando had described to him. Freckles made him think of daisies. Meadows and daisies.

"Oh, you may ask anything. Victor teaches me patience and humility, and whenever I think I've learned all there is to know of those subjects, he shows me I've really just begun." Adèle laughed.

"Yes," she said, "my pupils train me also, and I'm always amazed at what they know. But Victor, you had to teach him . . . everything."

206

"Exactly," said Itard. "Everything. But you see, it was from *him* that I had to learn how to do it."

"And because Victor has been such an excellent teacher," said De Gerando, "Jean-Marc has been elected to the new Legion of Honor, and the czar of all the Russias wants him as his personal surgeon. Come on, now . . . tell us about it!"

"Is it true," asked Madame De Gerando, "that he sent a gift with his invitation?"

"Victor," Itard called, "come here." The boy looked up from the knives, spoons, and forks. "Show Madame De Gerando the pin. The pin, remember?" Victor's eyes searched Itard's face as the doctor unbuttoned the boy's jacket. Something on his shirtfront caught the candlelight.

"Good lord!" said De Gerando. "It's a sapphire! I've never seen anything like it! My God, man—and you let Victor wear it? You're mad!"

"It's too gaudy," said Itard. "I don't like jewelry—it gets in the way. And I don't like honors, either; they also seem to get in the way. It's good to be appreciated, but the truth of it is, I'm only just beginning to accomplish something. The Russian ambassador received my humble thanks and my regrets. He would not take back the pin. Why would anyone want to go to Saint Petersburg? Their winter never ends, and we'll soon have a czar of our own in Bonaparte— though it seems only yesterday we got rid of a king. I have everything I need right here. The work I'm doing with the deaf children is fascinating and rewarding; my private prac- tice keeps growing despite all my efforts to contain it—and with Victor, something truly exciting has happened . . ."

He felt Adèle watching him. *I'm being too serious—too intense, as usual.*

"Please, Jean-Marc," said Madame De Gerando, "come follow Victor's example and tell us at the table. That is his special chair, Adèle. If we give him another, he sniffs them all till he finds it. Jean-Marc, you are next to Adèle, and, dear Victor, I will sit next to you, as usual." She took her seat. Victor alternately bounced and rocked. His hands were out of sight beneath the tablecloth.

"Maybe I should sit next to him," said Itard, starting up from his chair. "He's been especially difficult lately, more restless . . ."

"I can handle him, Jean-Marc; sit down, please."

"He reminds me of Robert," said Adèle. "He can't sit still either; and full of surprises. Today he asked me, 'Where is China?' And when I showed him on the globe he said, 'No! I mean where is China in *our* world?' Our world, I told him, is round, just like the globe. He laughed at me. 'No, it's not!' he said. 'You just think that because you are French!' "

"Yes!" said Itard. "That's it exactly. The world is *first* what one learns from the senses—that's where education begins!"

Victor patted the table, looking for something.

"Ah," said Madame De Gerando. "He needs his lentil plate." She rang her little bell. "Julie!"

Victor's gaze fixed on the opposite wall, then he was out of his chair and around the table; Itard had to twist his head to see what he was doing.

"Has he taken an interest in art?" asked De Gerando. "Do you like the painting, Victor?"

On his toes, the boy reached as high as he could and lifted a small oval picture from the wall; under glass, in a plain mahogany frame, a lake reflected some woods and mountains.

"It's one of mine," said Madame De Gerando, looking pleased. "A watercolor."

"It's an excellent picture," said her husband. "The color, the mood—Victor agrees."

Holding the picture before him, Victor trotted back to his place and, once seated, held it out horizontally toward the lentils.

"My God!" Madame De Gerando burst into laughter. "He wants it for a lentil plate! And I thought you were moved by my painting, Victor!"

"Well, he was, my dear," said her husband. "It's the one he chose to eat his lentils from, and you know how he feels about lentils." They were all laughing when Julie came in. "Please, Julie," said De Gerando, "bring Victor's lentil plate—or more pictures for the rest of us."

Not until the new plate was filled with lentils and set before him would Victor give up the picture. Itard replaced it on the wall.

"*This* is the exciting news," said Itard as he seated himself. "Our Victor has become an inventor! You have just witnessed the invention of the lentil plate. Only a few months ago I discovered—to my chagrin and great distress—that the words for everyday objects I had patiently taught Victor for over a year, to him meant *only* the specific objects that we used in our exercises; inadvertently, I had taught him that only *that* book was a 'book,' only *that* cup a 'cup' . . .

"Once I had realized this, it didn't take long to have him understand that the word 'book' applies to many objects that are similar, and *with* this—very naturally and easily—came adjectives: big, small, dark, light. In fact, he got the idea so well that all kinds of things became books. Not only *Candide* but the *Gazette* and pamphlets, even a handful of papers. A package of letters becomes a book—a picture becomes a plate, and Victor . . . becomes an inventor! Look at this . . ."

Itard reached into his jacket pocket and took out a small cylindrical object tied with string. "It may look to you like a piece of chalk stuck into a hollow skewer, but it's more precious to me than any sapphire; it's a chalk holder, and Victor invented it! When his chalk became too short to use, he thought of the skewer. He went to the kitchen and found it. The chalk fit, as you see . . ."

Itard held the thing out into the middle of the table and everyone leaned forward except Victor, who, neatly, efficiently, was consuming a second serving of lentils; from plate to mouth, forkful followed forkful.

"And then look! He tied it with a string so that it can't fall out. Man the inventor!"

"Dear Victor." Madame De Gerando tousled his hair. "I am so proud of you."

"To me," Itard continued, "this is momentous. Forgive

me if I seem to dwell on it, but with all the difficulties I've had—and continue to have—it marks what, I hope, is a turning point."

"Well, bravo!" said De Gerando, raising his glass. "To Victor the inventor!" Everyone raised a glass and repeated the toast, except for Victor. He blotted his lips with a napkin and then carried his water glass to a window facing the river. Itard glimpsed a rind of moon hurrying through tattered clouds. Victor gazed up at it and, holding his glass in both hands, took long, slow sips of water.

"Yes," said De Gerando thoughtfully, as he poured himself more wine. "Man the inventor: an important stage in human evolution. But there are, of course, higher and more important ones."

Itard looked at him. "You mean, of course . . ."

"Moral man," said De Gerando, nodding. "Man who understands right and wrong. Justice. This has been mankind's greatest struggle—as it still is, today."

Itard was silent for a moment. Then he nodded and raised his glass. "To moral man," he said. "To justice."

Coffee degerando! The steam rises into his eyes and nose. Coffee in little cups. One. Two. Three. Four.

"Very good, Victor. You didn't spill a drop. Here are the tray and the glasses for liqueur. We'll serve the coffee, and then I can go to my father. Do you remember Monsieur Guérin?"

Victor sees Victor in the tray.

"My father is dying, Victor. Do you know what that is?

No? Maybe someday you will . . . Now come, bring the tray."
Coffee degerando! One. Two. Three. Four.

"And now," said De Gerando, "the true confection of the evening. Adèle is going to sing us some of her English songs."

"They are Scottish," said Adèle, laughing. A flush of color tinted her cheeks and throat. English, thought Itard. I should learn it. He sipped the green liqueur, then the hot, inky coffee. I might ask her to teach me. De Gerando would be pleased, wouldn't he? De Gerando with freckles. Meadows and daisies.

Madame De Gerando was seated at the piano. Victor stood close and watched her face and arms.

"Maybe Adèle could teach you English, Jean-Marc," said the baron. "She's an excellent teacher—she could teach you to sing at the same time."

"English . . . perhaps," said Itard. "But please, Mademoiselle, *do* sing."

"Her name is *Adèle*, Jean-Marc," said Madame De Gerando, leafing through a book of music. "Which one would you like to do, my dear?" Adèle showed her the page and Madame De Gerando began to play. Adèle stood beside her, hands clasped. She opened her mouth and her voice startled Itard; surprisingly large, it set the air around his head quivering. Though music meant little to him—most concerts seemed a jumble of tooting and scraping that made staying awake difficult—he could follow a song. This one had an odd sound to it.

Victor watched Madame De Gerando's face and arms, but not her hands. He moved closer and paused, then closer yet. Reaching out, he patted her shoulder, and she half turned with a quick smile while continuing to play. He leaned forward, rested his cheek against her hair, and, with both hands, patted her shoulders.

"Dear Victor," she said, "it's very difficult to play when you do that." Victor put his arms around her and rubbed his face in her hair. The song was interrupted.

"Victor!" Itard quickly strode up and led the boy back to a chair between De Gerando's and his own.

"Does he like music?" asked Adèle.

"He seems indifferent to it. Do you like music, Victor?" Itard looked down at him, crouching next to De Gerando, whose knees he was patting.

"That's a good boy," said De Gerando. "Come sit now and listen to Adèle's song." Victor looked up, then rose and rubbed his forehead against the man's. De Gerando laughed.

"Victor! How affectionate you've become, but please, it's time to sit down." Hugging De Gerando tightly, Victor made small mewing sounds.

"Sit *down*, Victor," said Itard, "or we'll have to go." Victor showed his teeth. A smile? His eyes looked pained and close to tears. He patted Itard's hands and knees. Adèle, still near the piano, stared.

"I'm sorry, Adèle," said Itard. "Adolescence isn't easy for him."

"It isn't easy for *anyone*," said Adèle emphatically. She

reddened slightly. Madame De Gerando struck a chord on the piano.

"Let's start once more, Adèle; it was lovely." Adèle watched Victor slide his hands up and down his thighs. He suddenly seemed to see her. The piano began once more; Adèle nodded her head to the introduction, then released her strong, clear sound. Itard watched her shape it with her lips and teeth into discrete little packets. These words, he thought, mean as little to me as to Victor. Adèle's throat throbbed and pulsed. Her chest swelled, her breasts rose, and, clasping her hands in front of them, she directed her song at Victor, shaping the words more broadly, as if to make their meaning clear to him. Victor was still for a moment, his open mouth a circle.

Itard held Victor with an arm around the shoulders; the boy's hands began moving on his thighs more quickly now. Itard took hold of his wrists and stopped them, then patted his hands.

The song ended. Itard and De Gerando applauded and Victor trotted up to Adèle and took her hand.

"Victor!" Itard stood. "Come sit down!"

"It's all right . . ." said Adèle. She looked uncertain. "I think he wants to tell me he liked the song. Do you sing, Victor? You remind me of my Robert—of course, he's much smaller, but his eyes . . . are like yours. He likes to sing. He could teach you some songs. Does he have friends, Doctor? I mean, other children?"

"He's afraid of them," said Itard, beside them now. "They can be cruel and he avoids them. And of course, the children at the Institute can't speak, except with their signs. I've kept him away from them."

Victor patted Adèle's hand, then her forearm. He began pulling her toward an alcove near the door.

"Do you want to take me somewhere?" she asked him. "To show me something? Is it something you want to tell me?"

"Gentle, Victor, gentle . . ." said Itard. He and De Gerando stayed close.

"His eyes . . ." said Adèle, "his expression is so ardent—so urgent . . . What is it, Victor?" She allowed herself to be led into the alcove.

"Behave, Victor." Itard followed. "He's usually gentle, but sometimes, when he's upset, he can get very . . ." In the alcove, Victor circled Adèle slowly, still patting her arms. He was almost as tall as she. He looked into her face.

"Victor, Victor . . ." she said tenderly. Itard saw just a hint of fear. Victor touched at the fine waves and curls of her hair. "I can't tell," she said, "if you are sad or gay." She looked to Itard. "He's so . . . innocent, isn't he?" She laughed.

"Yes," said Itard, "absolutely innocent." He had no idea what Victor would do. He watched him put Adèle's hand to his cheek and rotate his face against it; then, laughing, he turned and offered his other cheek. Adèle caressed it, and after a moment Victor's eyes quivered and began to roll up. He shuddered all over.

"Victor!" said Itard, and the boy pushed away Adèle's hand and began galloping circles around her. She stood there stiffly. They all stood there, and Victor's shoes clattered on the parquet floor. The gallop slowed to a trot; he giggled and smiled at Adèle, then looked dismayed. Suddenly, with both arms, he embraced her and, with his head on her breast, he rocked her from side to side. His face twisted into a caricature of grief, and Itard found himself laughing and shaking his head. Victor's eyes swelled with tears and, roughly, he pushed Adèle away. A vase teetered and shattered on the floor.

"Oh, I'm so sorry," she said, her own tears welling.

"It's nothing, my dear," Madame De Gerando's arm was around Adèle's shoulders, and Itard had a firm hold of Victor, who was grinding his teeth with what seemed rage, while his body shook with sobs.

"It's my fault," said Itard over his shoulder. "I should have stopped him. Come, Victor—over here. It's all right, but you must be gentle." He led the boy to a chair in the hall, knelt in front of him, pressing his chest to the boy's knees, and firmly gripped his upper arms. The sobs continued.

"Gentle . . ." said Itard. "Gentle . . ." He winced at a flash of soldiers in a Toulon street, saw again things he never wanted to see.

"How do I teach you love between man and woman? What do I know of it? Victor, Victor . . . will you eventually become a sensible young man—take up a trade and find a wife? Some young thing from the woods?" He put his hand over the boy's forehead. It was cold and damp.

"Come, we'll go home—home to a bath. Come."

Victor was trembling. His face had become very pale. Two vivid streaks of blood emerged from his nostrils.

"How is he?" De Gerando put his hand on Itard's shoulder. "Oh my God, he's bleeding!" He knelt beside Itard and gave him his handkerchief.

"It's just a nosebleed," said Itard, blotting at it. "It happens when he goes wild; it seems to quiet him—or precede his quieting. I bleed him, too, but I can only do it so much. He's like this all the time; he has no peace. I can't continue much longer. After all our work, the savage is winning. Puberty. Sometimes I think I've educated him to see him become a lunatic—to see him locked up in Bicêtre, after all."

"It may *still* pass," said De Gerando. "When all the changes of puberty are complete, the social benefits will manifest themselves—tenderness, a preference for women— I'm sure of it."

"And moral man will spontaneously emerge? With each passing day, I doubt it more. This loving preference of men for women and women for men that nature, or God, has supposedly instilled in us seems to be lacking in many; when it comes to that 'tender emotion,' we are more like pigs than we care to know. And, meanwhile, puberty rages. Rages! I give him cold baths, I run him around the gardens, I bleed him and bleed him—he's completely mad with it! I have even considered finding him a prostitute." Itard looked into De Gerando's eyes and nodded gravely. "But the thought of what he might do with what he learns from her is too . . . terrifying."

De Gerando shook his head and looked at Victor; his face was gray, his mouth and chin smeared with blood, his staring eyes quivering, clouded over, seeing . . . what? De Gerando couldn't imagine.

30

Julie knocks and little Albert opens the door. His smaller cousin Lucas crawls up behind him and, from between Albert's legs, presents his snot-smeared face. "Aunt Julie! Aunt Julie! Mama's cooking a chicken! Come see the picture I made! It's a picture of that chicken! I made it!"

"Yes, how beautiful, it's a wonderful chicken. And, Lucas! How did you make your face so dirty? Is Grandmama here, Albert?"

"Yes, she's with Grandpa. I think he's sleeping some more. He's very sick, you know. He's dying. You know my friend Gérard? His father died."

"I know. I'm going to look in on Grandmama and Grandpapa for a while. Then I'll come and read you and Lucas a story." For children, she thinks, death is just another event, an adventure like everything else in their lives. Unless it comes too close. In the kitchen, Rose has been crying and Evelyn is nursing her youngest. Julie kisses them all and, as always, feels an impossible mix of relief and loss at Nicholas's absence. He has gone off to work in Lyon. She goes into the bedroom.

Her mother sits by the bed holding one of her father's hands clasped in both of hers. She pats and rubs it and Julie realizes that she has never seen her mother touch her father this way.

"Roger?" her mother says quietly from time to time. "Roger?"

Is this really her father? Has he died? Is it over? . . . But no—he makes a sound: raspy, from deep in his throat. A breath. He is sleeping, but his eyes are slightly open. Between the lids, she can see the whites, now yellowish, and even a bit of the pupil. His lips are stretched over the few teeth he has left. He looks so very old. No, not old: ancient, like someone who died long, long ago, and turned to parchment, to leather and bone. Her brother hadn't looked like this. Albert—the first Albert—was a baby, so soft and pale. She had been very little, but she remembers her mother's howl when they found him in his cradle, her mother cooking and weeping and scrubbing and weeping. Joseph, her oldest brother, had died before she was born. Before Evelyn, even. He was like someone in a fairy tale or legend; no one had seen him except Mama and Papa. There are so many dead.

Alicia, Violet, Louise: her dead cousins. Her little niece, Dominique. Her friends Marguerite and Emilie. Julie has had measles and fevers of all kinds. She has had croups and coughs and terrible cramps and vomiting and diarrhea but she did not die. She will not. Mama is never sick, except for her rheumatism sometimes. Most of the dead are children, and her mother insists they are in heaven.

"Heaven?" her father would say, and then wave toward the window—to Paris, to the street. "There's your heaven." And then his laugh, the way he laughs to show that something's not funny. Julie finds herself weeping.

The baby is crying, too, and Albert is singing something; a lullaby, but so loudly! "Albert, quiet!"—her sister in a loud whisper. "Grandpa is sleeping!"

"Roger?" her mother murmurs. "Roger?" Her father has been quiet for some time now. Her mother pats the pale hand. Julie stands behind and puts her hands on her mother's shoulders. She squeezes.

I am alive, Mama. I am alive.

31

In the near total darkness of the echoing street, Itard and Victor hugged the wall on their way home. Itard took a deep breath. He exhaled and was filled with gratitude at the relief of being alone. Now he could review the evening, try to make sense of it. A slight rain was falling, a kind of dripping mist, full of woodsmoke and the blended odors of all the kinds of offal and decay that gave Paris air its rich, strangely seductive character. Victor lifted his face to welcome it.

As always, on the very threshold of departure, with guests in coats and hats, De Gerando had begun a long anecdote. Victor tugged urgently at Itard's sleeve while Itard and Adèle told each other how glad they were to have finally met. Itard offered further apologies for Victor's behavior which Adèle insisted were unnecessary, and, while Victor trotted in place mewing, they arranged for her to visit the Institute the next Tuesday and lunch with Itard.

She seemed very pleased. There was a last round of thank-yous, the food and wine were praised once again, and, finally, the *final* good-nights.

Adèle.

"You liked Adèle, didn't you, Victor? She liked you, though you did frighten her a bit, poor thing; she's not used to you . . . Ah, Victor, Victor, what shall we do with you?"

She's all De Gerando had promised: wonderfully candid, obviously kind and loving, and bright—*very* bright, a woman's intelligence (a woman may be interested in philosophy, and discuss philosophy, but can never *be* a philosopher; why is that?). And she has a fresh, natural prettiness—meadows—that's rare in Paris. From the time I was a boy, after giving up the idea of joining the clergy, I have always assumed that at a certain point in my life, there would be a woman, a wife, and that she would be very like Adèle. And she's coming to have lunch with me. Dear De Gerando . . . *moral* man . . . *just* man . . .

As they crossed the bridge, the echoes of their footsteps seemed to double, and Itard realized that someone else was crossing also. His stomach tightened as he made out two dark, approaching masses, shapeless against the dark of night. He gripped both his walking stick and Victor, whom he pulled behind him, and continued cautiously along the opposite railing.

"Good evening, sir, though a bit of a wet one." At the sound of a woman's voice, Itard sighed and relaxed for a moment; then his throat tightened and went dry. The women crossed to his side of the bridge. "My daughter and I live just over the bridge; may we offer you a cup of tea and some . . . diversion?" The taller woman moved her face close to Itard's. Her teeth, exposed in smiling, floated luminous before him, as did her eyes. Her perfume was warm and lush: gardenia? rose?

"Is this your son?" asked the other one, who had been peering at Victor. He reached out, put his hands on her shoulders, and began to sniff her face.

"Oh Mama!" she giggled. "This one is funny! What *are* you doing, you funny thing? Is he simple, sir?" Itard couldn't see what, exactly, Victor was doing now, but the girl laughed and laughed.

"No, no, Victor . . ." he said. "We must go, I'm sorry, but . . ."

"Victor?" said the older woman. "Is this Victor the savage? Oh, sir, you *must* come and let us entertain you; my daughter is young—only fifteen—but she's very clever . . ."

"I truly *am*!" giggled the other. "Though not so clever as my dear mama. Please come, Victor! He wants to come!"

"Ladies, please! We *must* go home! Please!" Itard pushed past the two women, dragging Victor after him. Then, pushing Victor ahead, he hurried over the bridge and on into the lane on the other side.

"Another time, perhaps?" the older woman called after him.

"Good night, Victor! Good night, my sweet savage . . ." called the younger one. The echoes of their laughter and footsteps diminished, and Itard found himself breathless

and sweating profusely. My God! A mother and daughter!
He held fast to Victor's arm and, to escape the perfume
that seemed to pursue them, began to trot. It was raining
harder now. Alongside him, the boy skipped and leaped
again and again up into the pungent, misty shower.

32

The plates are on the shelf. The big plates. One. Two. Three. Victor takes the plates to the table. Madame Guérin's plate at Madame Guérin's place. Sausage and potatoes. Madame Guérin is cooking. This is Victor's plate. It smells of towel and shelf. Victor's chair smells of Victor. Monsieur Guérin's plate is chipped. His chair is old leaves and medicine and cold sweat. Sour and bitter. Monsieur Guérin is not here.

The bowls are on the shelf. One. Two. Three. The big bowls. One is Madame Guérin's. Sausage steaming, potatoes bubbling. Two is Victor's bowl. The ring goes round and round, smooth and shiny. Three. This is Monsieur Guérin's bowl. Monsieur Guérin is not here. Monsieur Guérin goes to work sometimes. He comes back full of earth, of sweat, of dead leaves. Of medicine sometimes. Shhhh, Victor. You must be quiet. Sometimes Victor must be quiet. Monsieur Guérin is sick sometimes. Sour and bitter and the bed is sour and bitter. The chamber pot fills the room, and medicine. Sometimes blood. This is Monsieur Guérin's place.

The forks are in the drawer. One two three. The spoons beside them. The big spoons. Soup. Victor looks into Madame Guérin's spoon, he sees a tiny Victor. He sniffs metal. On the table it touches Madame Guérin's plate. He sees another tiny Victor in Victor's spoon. He licks it. Metal. He puts it at Victor's place. Monsieur Guérin's spoon goes to Monsieur Guérin's place. Sour and bitter. And the forks. One. Two. Three. The table is set. The table hums. Victor hums.

Come, Madame Guérin. Come! The table is humming. Soup and sausage! Potatoes and bread! Madame Guérin is making noises again. Her face is behind her hands again. OHMYGOD ROGER! OHMYGOD ROGER ROGER ROGER! Victor pats her dress and apron. He smells the tears again. OHMYGOD OHMYGOD! Tears fill the kitchen, hot and steamy like water fills the tub. A tub of tears, OHMYGOD, on the soup and sausage, tears on the potatoes. Monsieur Guérin is not here.

Victor takes Monsieur Guérin's bowl from the table. He puts the bowl on the shelf. He puts Monsieur Guérin's plate on the shelf with the big plates. Victor takes Monsieur Guérin's spoon and fork. Victor puts them in the drawer. Victor shuts the drawer. Monsieur Guérin is not here.

ROGER ROGER ROGER. Madame Guérin is making tears and noises, warm, wet bread. Roger Roger. Madame Guérin velvet and Madame Guérin tears and soup and tears and potatoes.

33

2 *Frimaire, Year XIII*
(November 23, 1804)

My dear Adèle:

I must begin, once again, with apologies for not responding sooner to your delightful letters, so full, as always, of your sunny and vibrant good nature. That you have not heard from me over the preceding weeks has nothing to do with any fault of yours (if any fault you have; I am aware of none) but rather, as I've told you many times before, that particular fault of mine, which is my inability to limit the demands of my work, so as to leave me time to attend to other obligations.

I have initiated new efforts to have Victor learn to speak, as well as continuing with his other studies, in spite of his difficult behavior, which shows no signs, as yet, of improving. The work with the deaf children is much more promising, and takes more and more of my time, as does my private practice. Along with this, and my continuing research into the causes and potential cures of deafness, I have begun writing a paper outlining a theory I have regarding pneumothorax disease; and every day

the pile of unanswered letters on my desk continues to grow,
yours first among them. All this is to say, or rather, maybe, to
avoid saying, that I am a poor friend to you, not the one that
you deserve.

My dear Adèle, how can I say — explain — what must surely
have become obvious? I have never, before meeting you, attempted
to establish and nurture a friendship with a woman. I never
deeply questioned that I hadn't; it seemed simply that I hadn't
met anyone that inspired me to do so. You were the obvious and
perfect candidate, and I treasure the friendship that has
developed, but in coming to know you I have come to better know
myself, and what I have come to know, those truths that have
become so clear, are not always what we would choose. The most
painful truth I have had to face is that while for most people it
seems life is a matter of people (family, friends, etc.), for me it
is a matter of ideas; not that people are unimportant . . .

Itard put down his pen and rubbed his eyes and forehead
with the heels of his hands. This is absurd! This is no letter!

For weeks now, Itard had been avoiding the De Gerandos, who persisted in reminding him of how lovely, how
bright, how devoted Adèle was, and how unhappy he had
made her; just a letter, Jean-Marc, explaining your behavior . . . Poor Adèle! How does one tell a young woman—a
perfectly good, pleasant, decent, not unattractive young
woman—that one has no place in one's life for her? That
her conversation, while pleasant, is—to be honest—shal-

low and vapid and a bore! That one is not—whatever her charms—interested in her. The last time we were together, I had absolutely no desire to so much as hold her hand, and the idea of any more *intimate* physical contact is unthinkable! I have no desire to see her or write to her or hear of her. I tried, by God, I tried! The lunches, the dinners, the concerts, the endless walks and picnics . . . The more time I spent in her company, the greater my relief at leaving it. Marriage is a lovely idea, and it obviously suits the De Gerandos, but there are some—and I must be one—who were born for monasteries. How else to explain why she doesn't interest me . . . in *that* way? Or any other.

If it hadn't been for the Revolution, I would have taken vows. The puberty that drives Victor mad flared up in me and then seemed to vanish into a kind of . . . restless discomfort in the presence of women. How can I help Victor when I can't make sense of myself?

I have work to do! My work is my life and my wife; and Victor is the strange child of that marriage—and the deaf children. I don't lack for children, do I? The Institute is like a monastery full of children. If Victor won't speak to me, by God, they will!

Itard picked up his pen and a fresh sheet of paper.

Dear Adèle:

Thank you for your letters. I'm sorry not to have responded sooner, and, unfortunately, the continued pressure of work will make this reply brief. I cannot see on my calendar any opportunity

for a visit, either now or in the near future. Work keeps me in
Paris and leaves me no time for anything else. Please give your
parents my best wishes, and I hope this finds you in good health.
  Sincerely,
  Jean-Marc-Gaspard Itard

He stood up abruptly, folded the letter quickly and precisely, and sealed it.

"That's the end of it. I have work to do!"

34

The door is open.

This is the hall.

The stairs go down. Down the stairs past the boys. Laughing boys. Bad boys. Fingers, tongues, and teeth. Down the stairs and down the stairs and down the stairs.

Good morning, Victor. Where are you off to? The door is open. Outside there are birds. Outside.

Old Antoine sweeps. He sweeps on the cobbles with his big straw broom. Birds and leaves and light fly away. Victor smells the cool, wet stones and leaves. Little flowers. The sky is alight. The courtyard is shadow cool. Birds crash and screech in the bushes.

Old Antoine sweeps, he sweeps to the gate in the stony wall. The gate is open. The street. Antoine sweeps and leaves and twigs hop outside into the street and Victor is running. Old Antoine's eyes are round and milky, his mouth is round. His hands and fingers flap and flutter. Victor is running and it's the street.

Again and again shoes strike the stones, again and again and into the wind. Big eyes in a hairy face, the mouth says Victor and it's gone. The wind. The wind is humming in Victor's hair and ears, cool like water, humming like water—Victor's hand! Madame Guérin is not holding Victor's hand! The doctor sits in his black suit scratching words. Look here, Victor. No, Victor! No! Look here! Victor is running.

Victor is running. His face and chest strike black cloth, the cobbles spin and strike his head; a bucket rolls and rattles. There is screaming and warm milk. He sees the sky full of light and birds. He licks milk from his lips and stands up, he slips in milk, he slides and runs from the screaming woman. He sucks milk from his sleeves and runs.

Birds screech and bounce in the gutter. He runs and runs. Here are flowers and leaves just beginning. The Gardens! The Gardens! The Luxembourg Gardens! Madame Guérin! Madame Guérin is not holding his hand. Look here, Victor. It's time to look here. Again, Victor, try it again! Babies. Nurses and milky babies. Look at the baby, Victor. Look how sweet. Victor is running, Victor is flying, he's slip-skidding in what horses drop and his mouth is full of stone. He claws and scrambles, and he's running, gravel and salt on his tongue.

He runs through the thick stink of horse and burning wood, through a warm wave of bread and rotten dead things and blood. He runs through a cloud of cheese and horse again, always horse and burning wood. He's running in wind, through wind, a wind full of trees, many trees and wet earth and old leaves and he runs faster. Victor sees the big big wall. This is the big big wall, Victor. Victor runs through the big big gate and his shoes strike earth again and again. Light dazzles and spatters the trees and a girl with large eyes shouts and is gone.

Trees fly past and around. Their rough skin strikes and scrapes his outspread palms. His feet pound the carpet of leaves and up come gusts of rotten acorn and beetles, worms and mushrooms. He smells new ferns among the roots and he's on his knees, snapping off the crisp stalks, crunching and chewing, his mouth full of succulent greenness.

He is in motion. Trees fly past, this way and that and a turn of his head brings a whiff of water, sparkling and gurgling, and he's running to water; he hears it and he laughs. His feet beat the spongy earth and water splashes on rocks and pebbles. Icy water splashes his face, his tongue. He slides into it, under it. It surrounds him, roaring and shouting, and he swallows again and again and again. He is water.

He is awake. He smells trees. Where is Madame Guérin? Above are trees. And this way trees, and this way also. He feels among the stones and moss. Where is Victor's blanket? He searches wet pockets. Jacket pockets, trouser pockets, where is Victor's bowl? The bowl is on the shelf. The milk is in the pitcher. He finds what is between his legs. He holds it, he pulls it. It will not go away. Madame Guérin is in the kitchen. Milk and bread. He is moving, he is running. His shirt is cold, and his trousers try to hold him. His jacket grasps his arms. He runs through green, around trees, and there are no bowls. Here is a mushroom, and here and here. Again and again in his pockets there are no bowls. The bread is on the shelf. He sees it and he runs. It's time to go home, Victor.

He's rolling, over and over, twigs and branches snapping, over the stones and moss and roots. Mud. Victor's hands are full of mud. Where is Victor's towel? Madame Guérin. Madame Guérin is not here! The towel is on the shelf. One foot is big, one foot is small. One has a shoe and one has none. Where is Victor's shoe? It's time to go home. It's time to set the table. It's time for work. Let us begin, Victor. Try it again, Victor. No, Victor! Try it again! No! No! No!

Cold and wet. Something touches his face. Again. And again on his head, in his eyes. He turns his face up, mouth open. Rain. It touches his tongue, it touches his teeth. He sees the drops flying down to his eyes, and he's spinning round and round, catching rain in his hands and mouth and all around he hears the leaves—tap tap tapping. And more leaves, and more and more, drumming and battering and he spins falling and curling so the rain can cover him and wrap him and warm him. It's time to go home. Lentils and sausage. Milk.

Where is Victor's blanket? He holds what is between his legs. Victor? Where is Victor? It's time, Victor. It's time to cut the wood. Sawing and sawing and sawing. Wood clatters on the floor and Victor laughs. He pulls what is between his legs, he pushes it. He squeezes it, he shakes it. He wants it and he wants it. It will not go away. In his closed eyes he sees L–A–I–T, he sees T–A–S–S–E, he sees V–I–C–T–O–R.

Once again, Victor. Bring me the scissors—*No!* Bring me the thimble—*No!* Bring me the cup—*No!* That's terrible! That's *terrible*! *No! Victor, no!*

He's awake. Darkness. This is not Victor's bed. Milk. It's time for milk. Madame Guérin! Things are moving. Leaves are hissing. There are trees. There is no fire. Madame Guérin! Milk. The earth sinks and sucks at his feet. Dead leaves, rotting leaves. The black trees move this way and that. Madame Guérin! Whispers hiss above and around him. Whispering leaves hissing and hissing and now they are roaring. The wind. The wind! Light leaps and blows down from the leaves—running and running. From under leaves, cold and wet, acorns are bitter and musty. Running and running. Madame Guérin!

Smoke. Burning wood. His mouth fills with water. It's time to go home. Sawing and sawing, the wood clatters. Into the fire. The pot and the warm milk. The table, the bowl. Lentils and sausage. Madame Guérin!

Light flares day through the trees. The sky! Black hills. A house. A house and smoke. Milk and bread and Victor's bowl. The wind slaps at him, slaps his jacket. The earth is soft and deep. He falls. He runs and falls. Madame Guérin! A dog barks and barks and barks. Teeth. He smells chickens. Eggs and bread. He hears chickens. Time to go home, Victor. Set the table. He's running. Here is a house. Here is another. Milk and bread. Woodsmoke fills his mouth with water again and again.

Barking! Growling, teeth snapping! Children! He smells children! People and running and shouting. People running. Victor runs. Runs through shouts. Shouts and screams. Eyes and mouths and teeth and screams. Hands!

Men. Dark coats stink of old wine. Piss and sweat. They talk into his face. They have big teeth. Some have hair all over. They talk and talk. Bread fills his mouth. Bread and bread and bread. Sausage! Milk in a metal cup. Where is Victor's bowl? This is not Victor's room. Where is Victor's bed? Victor's blanket? This is straw and this is straw. Victor goes under the straw. Men come to the gate and talk and talk. Water in a metal cup. Taste the metal. Victor goes under the straw. He holds what is between his legs. He closes his eyes, he rocks and rocks, he sees Madame Guérin. He smells her hands and hair. Her damp apron full of flour. Her velvet dress.

35

27 Germinal, Year XIII
(April 17, 1805)

Itard opens the window; a tepid breeze dabs at his face and throat. The rain that, for over a week, has drenched and flooded Paris seems, finally, to have ended. There, over the Luxembourg Gardens, a rift in the clouds shows blue sky. He has just finished his notes on the experiment with the Michaud boy. The insertion of the catheter, pouring the infusion into the ear. My God, the boy had screamed! This was his second experiment in trying to restore hearing. The boy had screamed for quite a while, but finally quieted. The inner ear is very sensitive. Fever had developed after about half an hour. The boy was sleeping when Itard left him in the infirmary.

In the two weeks that Victor has been missing, Itard has immersed himself in his work with the deaf children. The police were searching Paris, and authorities in the surrounding towns and suburbs had been supplied with descriptions, and although Madame Guérin kept insisting more must be done (she spent her days combing the streets all around the Institute), what more *could* be done? One could only pray he'd be found unharmed. She blames me, and with good reason. I am to blame.

Even before this, over the year since her husband died, she has been more and more openly critical of Itard's work with Victor: you're too hard on him; you push him and push him; leave the boy be . . . And with frustration and fading hopes, Itard began to think she might be right; if he could just accomplish one last thing . . . Oh, Victor! How stupid of me! What vanity! Itard flexes his bandaged, bitten hand, the left. Although the swelling is gone, it's still sore. The bite. Victor, Victor, our work is over . . . It's finished.

This morning the message came from central Guard Headquarters: a few days ago, a boy of Victor's description had been caught in a village near Passy and, after confirming the identification, had been brought back to Paris. He is alive and apparently intact, and Madame Guérin, in spite of her rheumatism, has rushed off to fetch him home.

A few weeks before Victor ran away, Itard had finally faced several facts: First, that Victor's progress in the past year had been imperceptible. Second, that Victor would never speak. (Had Pinel been right after all? The suspicion infected his thinking and jeered his efforts.) If ever speech was possible, that time had passed. And, third, that the puberty he'd been struggling with all these years could well be a permanent state of violent hysteria. The only thing Itard hadn't tried was the one thing he believed would really help: revealing to the boy, in one way or another, the source and aim of his tormenting desires. This, after endless, anguished inner debate, Itard realized he could never do. It was time to end their work.

He weighed his real achievements: the tremendous distance Victor had come from the creature he had been. He had learned invention, and understood language. He could read and write a small vocabulary. He was a social being. He was truly human. A person. Or was he? What really distinguishes humanity? Over and over he heard De Gerando intoning, "What of *moral man*? What of the sense of *justice*?" Yes. If that has been achieved, we have accomplished something essential, something profound. I would be satisfied. But how could he test for this sense?

In the past, Victor had been punished for things—stealing food, mostly—at first with the blow of a ruler across his palms, which only made his stealing more furtive, then by being deprived of treats he especially loved; this was more effective. He no longer stole. But was it simply fear of punishment? Was there any understanding of the nature of sin, and therefore justice? Itard had also punished him sometimes for doing poor work by locking him in his room. He always accepted these punishments passively; was it because he believed them just?

Itard's hand begins to throb. The bite. They had been working well that day. Victor had been extraordinarily calm. He had copied on his slate every word on Itard's list. The letters were mostly recognizable; almost anyone could have read them, and Itard had praised him all morning.

Suddenly, with a frown and an angry shout, Itard erased all the boy's work, threw his books and chalk across the room—as he did sometimes when he was *truly* angry—and he started to pull Victor out of his office, and down the hall to the little windowless closet under the stairs in which, during his first weeks at the Institute, they used to lock him.

When Victor understood what was going to happen to him, he did what he had never done before: he fought. Kicking and clutching the door frame in whatever way he could, he fought. And inwardly Itard exulted—yes, Victor! Fight!—but continued to push him into the little prison. And when Victor saw that with all his screams and strength he could not save himself, he bit Itard's hand and the blood spurted. The pain was sudden and intense. Itard screamed and slapped at Victor's clamped, grinding jaws again and again, blood spattering, until finally the boy released him and stood facing Itard, chest heaving, red teeth bared; his blood- and tear-smeared face crumpled with pain, grief, and rage; his eyes huge and incredibly open.

And with a plunge of vertigo, Itard stared into the abyss of Victor's life, his soul; he teetered at its edge, and looked down past torn, jagged edges through layers and layers of countless disappointments and hideous betrayals: scars over scars over scars, now all ripped open and gaping.

Then Victor was gone, clattering down the hall and up the stairs, Itard after him, and the mad chase through the apartment and then down again, through the classrooms and out into the courtyard, where old Antoine finally cornered him, and Itard got hold of him again. Itard held him firmly with every effort at gentleness, and Victor went limp, pale, and silent, and though he seemed not to be weeping, tears ran from his eyes. He let the doctor carry him back upstairs through the silence of the deaf, past the open mouths and eyes, back up to the apartment where Madame Guérin rushed to meet them. Victor clung to her, his face buried in her apron as if it were her womb he wanted. She embraced him and rubbed his head and back while she looked at Itard in horrified disbelief.

"What have you done?" she said. "What have you done?"

In the following week, Itard did everything he could think of to make Victor understand that it had been an experiment, that Victor was right and good—even to have bitten him—and that he himself had been wrong, and was truly sorry and would never test him like that again. Not ever again. But Victor would not look at him. He had achieved the stature of moral man. He knew justice and injustice. Itard stood convicted and condemned. And then Victor disappeared.

Oh God! How could I have been so stupid! Why did I have to prove what I already should have known? And the irony was that it was Itard—teacher, doctor, scientist—who had brought the boy to this level, raised him to this awareness. What an irony! The pain of it tore him, it chewed at him; he woke with it, walked with it, and lay down with it. How stupid he had been! And so, he turned to the deaf children.

Now he could devote himself to them. Now he could see even more clearly how long it had been since his work with Victor had shown any progress. Victor was all he would ever be. But the deaf children could be taught. They could be brought to full humanity. Already, there were two who could speak and understand speech and would leave the Institute to join the greater world. And he would continue to search for a cure for deafness. The new infusion was promising, and he'd heard of work being done with electricity in Italy. Now he was free to pursue every avenue . . .

He hears Madame Guérin's voice in the entryway, the voice she uses with Victor. He hears them move through the apartment, the familiar, little quick-steps that were still a trot—Victor has really never learned to walk like other children—Madame Guérin's murmur, leading him to his own room, surrounding him with her voice and her love and its promise of absolute sanctuary, the warm, mossy hollow where one can curl and sleep safe. Two weeks wandering God knows where—woods, fields—what is he like? Stripped of all they had accomplished? Returned to what he was? Stupid! So stupid of me!

There is silence. She is getting him settled. Itard looks to the window. The city is steaming into the hazy new sunlight. He flexes his hand until it hurts and tears blur the view. Paris! This vile dunghill where people with their bricks and smoke and stink obscure the spring-greened hills. He waits for the tapping on his door.

The tapping comes and she enters the room. Her face is closed to him. It would always be closed to him now.

"The police had him in a cage full of dirty straw and shit," she says. "Thank God he's alive. He's very thin and very dirty. They didn't wash him once. When he saw me he went white—in spite of the dirt, absolutely white—and he fainted. His eyes rolled up and he fell on the floor like an empty sack. I held him and they revived him with salts. He opened his eyes and shrieked with joy. I thought he would break my bones. He sniffed me and patted me all over. He cried and cried with snot pouring out of his nose. They had me sign some papers; they gave me these for you to sign." She gives him the sheaf in her hand. "In the carriage he clung to me and hid his face in my breast; even when we arrived in the courtyard, he wouldn't look at anything. The boys greeted him, they waved: Hello, Victor—you know how they do. They always want to talk to him, to play with him. I don't know why you've never let them. It wasn't till we were in the apartment that he looked around, began to touch things—the little table near the door, the vase— then down on the floor sniffing the rug, the curtains, the windowpanes. He ran to the kitchen, snatched his bowl from the shelf, and drank a whole bucket of milk, and then he pulled me to his room. He found his blanket and wrapped it completely around his head and crawled into bed—into a ball. I tried to get him up to wash him. He's filthy. But I couldn't. He's there, rocking."

Her face is flat and smooth like a wall. Her eyes two shuttered windows.

"I'll go in," he says. "You know my work with him is finished. For a long while now there's been no progress. I've made mistakes. This last incident was one of the worst; it was wrong. I had no idea he would react so strongly—but I'm glad he did. It's to his credit. He has a sense of justice and I'm very proud of that. That was the point, you see." Her jaw tightens as he speaks, and continues to tighten.

"I know you think I've overworked him; I know what you think. But try to understand, I've had to feel my way, always groping for the next step, and it wasn't the work that upset him—*believe* me, I have anguished over it—it's this madness we call puberty that goes on and on and gives us no peace! The truth is, Victor's . . . presence here has become more and more disruptive. Yes, maybe at some point he could have profited from more interaction with other children. If they had been normal children, there's no question that it would have been beneficial; but they being deaf, and he being . . . Victor . . ."

"They could have spoken!" She blurts it out and startles him. "He can always tell me what he wants, and so can they; they don't need words!"

"Exactly! The very reason I decided against it. They use signs. I wanted him to speak, just as I want them to. He never will; he was alone . . . too long, but because of all my work with Victor, I have no doubt that the deaf can be taught to speak. I've done it . . ." She was no longer looking at him.

"In any case . . . I have spoken to Sicard about some new arrangements. There is a small house around the corner: 4

246

Impasse des Feuillantines. It belongs to the Institute. You and Victor can live there. We—the Institute and the Ministry of the Interior—will provide for you so that you can continue to care for him. There's ample room for Julie, if you'd like to have her with you. The house needs a bit of work, some fixing up. I can do much of it . . . Victor can help, too. I'll go and see him now."

She nods—"Thank you, Doctor"—and turns to go.

"Sophie," he says, maybe the first time he has addressed her by her first name. "You are a very wonderful woman. All you have done, all you have given him; you have been a mother and more . . . much more."

"More?" she says. "What more is there?"

"I did my very best," he says. "In many ways I failed, but I did all I could possibly . . ."

"It was too much," she says, "and it was not enough." The door closes and she's gone.

Itard looks up at the shelves. His teaching machines: the blackboard with pegs from which to hang things and spaces below for the chalked words; the alphabet board with its compartments and cutout letters; the board of shapes and colors . . . He had done his best. This world is a world of things: tools, pots and pans, furniture, buildings, words and ideas . . . my God, what a clutter. What is it we really need? What is it we really are?

He goes down the hall to Victor's room and taps on the door as he always does. Then he goes in.

"Victor," says Itard. He sits on the bed. "Hello, Victor. I'm so glad you've come back." The boy lies on his side, his knees pulled up to his chest, arms and hands held deep between them. His blanket encloses his entire head in a huge turban. He rocks back and forth, back and forth. "I'm so very glad to see you, Victor. There will be no more work now. It's finished. You've done well. I am privileged to have been your teacher." Itard reaches up under the blanket, finds the back of the boy's neck, and begins to knead it gently, as he used to, in the first years. "Being a human being," he says, "what could be more difficult? You are an excellent boy, Victor, such a good, dear boy."

One of the boy's hands slips from between his legs and reaches up under the blanket to Itard's hand, pulls it to his eyes, and holds it there. Gradually, the rocking subsides. They sit like this for a long time.

36

TWO BREADS

CABBAGE

ONIONS

GARLIC

CHESTNUTS

LENTILS

OIL

Victor has the oil bottle. The bottle is in the basket. The coins are in Victor's hand. Hold them tight. Walking past the gardens. The bars. See the trees. Trees, bar, trees, bar, trees, bar . . . Leaves are falling. Leaves are flying. Leaves skitter and tumble down the street. Shoes can crunch them. Smell of old leaves. Dead leaves and other dead things. The wind blows the light. It's blowing now. See the ladies in the gardens. Nurses and babies. Look how sweet. The sky is soft and gray. Victor's scarf. Victor is going to the grocer.

Victor is going to the baker. Two breads. Cabbage soup with bacon. With onion. Chestnuts chestnuts.

"Good day, Savage. How is Madame Guérin today?"

The man that smells of sweat and coffee. Faces. Mouths and whiskers and the smell of whiskers.

"Watch out for the carriage, Savage!"

Mud. Carriages can splash you. Carriages can hurt you. Horses can hurt you. Big horses. Dogs can hurt you. Teeth. Victor helps Madame Guérin. Victor is a good boy.

"Good morning, Savage." The lady that smells of cats and potatoes and cheese. Watch out for the wagon! Wagons can hurt you. A wagon of wood. Smell the wood. Victor cuts wood for Madame Guérin. He saws it and saws it and saws it, and it falls. Victor laughs. He's a good boy.

"Do you think we'll get a bit of sun today, Savage?" The lady that smells of flowers and fish. "Would you like that? We all could do with a bit more sun. Give my best to Madame Guérin. Do you ever hear from Julie? Do you remember Julie?" Flowers and fish. A bit of sun. Sun on the stones. On the walls on the windows. The wind! It blows the light! It blows the leaves and the light! Smell the river! Fast water, too much water. Deep and fast. Smell it!

"Look! It's the old Savage chasing leaves! Maybe he's got some money. Hey, Savage! Here, Savage, Savage. Come on, monkey. Bald old monkey! Have you got some money for us? Don't run away . . . you're too fat! We can catch you! Hold him, Maurice! He's so fat! What's in your hand? Open it! Open it, monkey, or I'll twist your fingers off!"

"You boys leave him alone! François! You should be

ashamed, Maurice! All of you . . . your mothers will hear of this! Come in, Victor. Come in. It's all right, it's all right . . . How are you? And Madame Guérin? Is she well?"

Smell the onions and rotten cabbage and dust and butter and cats and potatoes and thyme and oil and cats. Cats. "What can I give you? Cabbage? That's a good one. Smell it, it's good. Garlic. Onions. Is this enough chestnuts? I'll fill your oil bottle. Anything else? You're not forgetting anything? Would you like an apple? Here's an apple for you. Do you ever see the doctor? We see him, he walks by sometimes—with his cane now, poor man. Arthritis, I think. A great man. Helping those deaf children to hear—to talk. To be citizens. Yes, many of them learn to talk a bit. They come in here sometimes. You don't like to talk, do you, Victor? Well, that's all right, you can read, you can write some words . . . What are you writing on your slate? L–A–I–T? You've got your cup? Jean, give the savage a cup of milk. Yes, the doctor's a great man. He made you a citizen like all the rest of us. Do you know that? I remember when you first came—I was just a little girl. They had you on a leash! Do you remember that? Now you are a citizen—a Parisian, a Frenchman! Don't you forget it. That's something to be proud of. And here . . . don't forget your basket. Goodbye. Goodbye, Victor!"

Wind. Windy. The leaves are flying. The light is blowing away. The wind is blowing the sun away. The wind is blowing Victor away. Away. Away with the wind and the light and leaves.

Victor is a good boy.

37

April 8, 1828

All morning I've been haunted by the most absurd and disturbing dream. What am I to do with it? What does it tell me? It was probably inspired by my seeing Victor yesterday, the first time in almost a year. I watched him from across the boulevard; he was out with a basket on a shopping errand, scurrying gnome-like, hunched and frightened. He's become even fatter. I remembered my first sight of him: a wild forest sprite. My God, what time does to us. Youth and strength, which we cannot but believe an endless fountain, are spent like any inheritance, and after a lifetime of striving, the only certain reward is suffering and death. Even writing is becoming more and more painful.

In my dream I felt no pain, and I thought, Praise God! I'm cured! I was out walking on a beautiful spring day, strolling through a meadow full of wildflowers toward a stand of birches. A well-dressed couple emerged from the trees; at first I thought is was the De Gerandos. Then I realized the man was Victor, top-hatted, young, and handsome, as he always is in my dreams—by God, I must dream of him at least once a week. They approached and came quite close before I saw that the woman with him was Julie Guérin! It's been years since I've seen or heard or thought of her.

Julie greeted me with a warm smile, but Victor was reserved and formal. His eyes, as always, were sad, and as always, I felt guilty for not having visited him all these years.

"Good afternoon, Doctor," he said. "It's been so long since we've seen you. Do you know we've had a baby?"

"I had no idea," I answered. "Congratulations to both of you!" And then I noticed the large baby carriage. "May I see it?" I asked, peering in.

"Why, of course," said Julie. "We've named him after you," and she lifted out an infant all in lacy white with a frilly white bonnet, and held it lovingly up for me to see.

It was myself! An infant, but with my puzzled, unhappy face. It looked up and stared at me and then its little mouth began to quiver and it began to cry.

I woke with tears streaming down my face, my chest full of that mix of joy and pain, hope and hopelessness, that brings the tears.

After all my years of work, first with Victor and then with the deaf, keeping them from signing and trying to force speech out of them, it has finally become clear to me that signing is their natural and valid language, and one that I have never bothered to learn. Victor might have

253

learned to speak with his hands. Maybe easily. He might have had conversations, friends. He might have learned stories, told jokes. Learned to pray. And what might have become of him then?

38

4 *Impasse des Feuillantines*
Paris, France
April 10, 1828

Julie Guérin
17 Emberley Street
London, England

Dear Julie:
  We buried Victor this morning. I am bereft. Last Tuesday he woke as usual. He made the fire. He coughed a bit but ate well. He did a bit of shopping. My legs are bad. Wednesday he did not get up. I went to see. I found him on the floor by his bed. I am bereft. I sent a message to the Doctor. I have not seen him at all for 2 maybe 3 years. He did not come. Nor to the funeral. He's never come. I've had no news from Rose in Lyon. Evelyn has croup. The children are fine. Albert and Lilly are in Lyon also. I think she is pregnant. I am bereft. Come home, Julie. You can teach here. You could still marry. It's time to come home.
  Your mother,
  Sophie Guérin

Victor must have been close to forty years old when he died
of unknown causes in the spring of 1828.

Doctor Itard became increasingly well-known for his
work with the deaf. He published many influential books
and articles, including a two-volume work, *Treatise on Dis-
eases of the Ear and Audition,* which was considered authoritative for many years. His two reports on his work with
Victor were published by the Ministry of the Interior, and
they inspired and influenced, among others, Maria Montessori. Montessori was deeply moved and impressed with
Itard's reports, translated them into Italian, and used many
of his ideas and techniques to develop the method of edu-
cating children that bears her name. Many believe that
Itard, through his work with Victor, invented special education; methods similar to his are used in teaching the de-
velopmentally disabled and those with learning disabilities.

Itard continued to live in his apartment at the Institute

for Deaf-Mutes until a long and painful unnamed illness forced his retirement to Passy—at that time a rustic sub-urb of Paris—where he spent his last days gardening and doing a bit of carpentry. He died in 1838 at the age of sixty-three. He never married.

As for Madame Guérin and Julie, I know nothing more.